Books by Crissy Smith

Were Chronicles

Pack Alpha
Pack Enforcer
Pack Territory
Pack Rogue

Shifter Chronicles

Birds of Prey
Bear Claw
Eye of the Tiger
Coyote's Kiss
Wolf Pack
Lion's Claim

Bloodlines

Bite
Control

Anthologies

What's Her Secret?

Single Titles

Designated Alpha

Lion's Claim

ISBN # 978-1-78686-156-6

©Copyright Crissy Smith 2017

Cover Art by Posh Gosh ©Copyright 2017

Interior text design by Claire Siemaszkiewicz

Totally Bound Publishing

Published in 2017 by Totally Bound Publishing, Think Tank, Ruston Way, Lincoln, LN6 7FL, United Kingdom.

Shifter Chronicles

LION'S CLAIM

CRISSY SMITH

Dedication

This one is for all the Shifter Chronicles fans who were ready and waiting for a new book and sent happy thoughts as I decided how I wanted to approach the next few stories.

Chapter One

The alarm shrieked, scaring Annabelle Sanchez awake and out of bed. She stumbled around the room, dressing quickly. This wasn't the first time and wouldn't be the last that her morning started that way, but it always made her leap up in fear. Her bedside clock read three-fifteen a.m. Having been taught to always be prepared, Annabelle jogged down the hall less than four minutes after the warning call. Doors opened as she passed, signaling others rushing to join her.

Mac Gordon was on his phone as Annabelle ran into the main bar area, Trent, Carter and Kelly spreading out behind her. Trent and Carter each stood next to one of the windows to peer out while Kelly ran to take position by the front door. Annabelle's place was at Mac's side. She would carry out all Mac's orders while directing the rest of the team.

The rumble of motorcycles shook the floorboards where she stood and she recognized the sound of those pipes. At normal times, Annabelle would be comforted by the people who were arriving, but in the middle of the night, with the alarms still ringing, she was filled with dread. There was no reason for two of the team to be coming in hot.

"They're here," Mac said into his cell. "Put everyone else on high alert. We'll take care of things here. Good job."

Mac's words had everyone in the room tensing. Putting the entire town on high alert was a big deal. The town of Brookside had around two hundred residents only, mostly shifters or their loved ones. It was a unique place but perfect for the secrets that had to be kept.

Annabelle wiped her hands down the legs of the sweatpants she'd pulled on. Her heart still pounded. It'd be a long morning and she'd only been in bed for a few short hours.

Mac turned toward them. "We have an emergency case," he said.

"Trouble?" Trent asked. He bounced on his toes as though he itched to get into the thick of things.

"No signs of it so far," Mac told him before glancing at Kelly. "Kelly, can you make some food? They're going to be hungry."

"Of course," Kelly replied, already hurrying toward the kitchen.

"Trent, Carter," Mac said. "Take your bikes and backtrack to the south. Make sure no one followed."

"You got it, boss," Trent responded with a wide grin.

Annabelle knew that he hoped to actually find someone following, and had to shake her head. The hyena shifter was just a little bit crazy at times. Trent gave a quick nod to Carter and the two men stalked toward the back door to follow orders.

"What's going on?" Annabelle asked once she and Mac were alone.

"Not sure," Mac confessed. "Calvin and Duffy have someone with them. Since they didn't call me first, we have to proceed cautiously."

The motorcycles' engines cut off and Annabelle took the time to brace herself for what would be coming through the doors. In the many years she'd worked along with Mac, there hadn't been much she hadn't seen. It was sad to say that nothing surprised Annabelle any longer. People, human or shifter, could be so cruel to one another.

The front door opened and Calvin Montgomery stepped inside first. A young woman with long, flowing red hair had practically attached herself to him. Duffy followed behind the two, pulling the door shut before moving to lean against the wall.

From the front, the bar wasn't much to look at, sure. But as an establishment that welcomed some rough characters nightly, its rundown exterior meant one thing—that whoever set foot inside would be comfortable.

Tabletops might be scarred and the floor scratched, but so what? The important thing about it? That a person's species didn't matter when they walked inside the Den. Everyone was invited to sit and enjoy a good brew.

The woman with Calvin didn't look like she'd ever stepped into a place like their bar before, but that was all right. She wouldn't be on the main floor for long.

Annabelle did her best to appear as non-threatening as possible while taking a few short steps forward. She didn't know the girl's story, but, like all the shifters who came through the Den, this woman needed the kind of help only they could offer.

"Samantha," Calvin said softly. "Annabelle is the one I was telling you about. She'll get you settled."

Annabelle smiled at the redhead. She had beautiful clear green eyes, and freckles across her nose. She couldn't be much older than twenty. "It's nice to meet you, Samantha." She kept her voice gentle.

"Hello," Samantha replied, peeking around Calvin.

"I bet you could use a good meal, a shower and bed." Annabelle waved her hand around. "It might not look like much, but you'll be comfortable here, I promise."

Samantha nodded at her and glanced at Calvin.

"You go ahead with Annabelle," Calvin told her. He motioned to Mac. "That's my boss. I have to tell him what's going on."

"O…okay." Samantha looked at Mac nervously.

Mac might have appeared intimidating with his dark hair and eyes, along with his full beard. A huge, muscular, tattooed biker, to Annabelle he was also the kindest man she'd ever met. Mac smiled encouragement at Samantha. It normally didn't take their guests long to trust him, so Annabelle felt certain that Samantha would soon be one of

Mac's biggest fans.

"I can already smell Kelly's cooking," Annabelle said, pulling Samantha's attention to her.

"I am hungry," Samantha admitted, her voice small.

"Well, then," Annabelle said. "Follow me." She led the way out of the main room and past the bar area. Since the bar had closed up hours ago, all the neon signs had been turned off and only a few security lights remained on. Samantha wouldn't ever be in the public part of the bar again. Once through the doors, she'd be kept out of view from anyone who might stumble in or come looking for her.

Behind her, Mac greeted Calvin and Duffy. The back-slapping was boisterous. Calvin and Duffy had been gone two weeks, which wasn't unusual. They loved to travel around on their bikes and, if they weren't needed at home, they might be anywhere in the US. Annabelle envied their freedom, but she had her own reasons for never leaving their small northern California town.

"Hi!" Kelly greeted them warmly as they stepped into the open kitchen.

The space wasn't big and a large stainless-steel oven and fridge dominated the room, but it was inviting. Annabelle always felt warm and comfortable there. While the bar did sell some appetizers and easy items, the real cooking took place once the doors were closed to the public. During the day, Kelly worked as a waitress along with Annabelle, but Kelly loved to cook for the family.

"It smells good," Annabelle praised. "This is Samantha."

"Hi, Samantha." Kelly waved. "Make yourself at home at the table. I'll have something to snack on here in just one minute. I also made a fresh pot of coffee."

"Thank you," Samantha replied quietly. "I hope you didn't go to too much trouble."

"Nah," Kelly said. "I'm glad Calvin and Duffy are back. Plus they brought you, so it gives me an excuse to cook."

Annabelle smiled as she pulled out a chair for Samantha from the table. None of the chairs matched, but that didn't matter. This was where all of the family ate meals together, so there was plenty of room—especially when they never knew who from town might drop by. Kelly really did love cooking for the people she cared about. Before she had joined them, Kelly had cooked in a restaurant, working fourteen or more hours a day. Now she only stood behind the stove when she wanted to.

"Can I get you something to drink?" Annabelle asked Samantha.

When Samantha sat in the chair, with Annabelle still standing behind her, Annabelle picked up the scent of dirt and foliage. *Fox shifter.* Annabelle was surprised. Foxes weren't a very common shifter species and she'd only ever met one other. Annabelle didn't say anything to Samantha about it, though. It wouldn't be comfortable for her to be around such large predatory shifters. Since her own animal was rare and small, Annabelle hoped Samantha would be even more at ease in her presence.

The way Samantha kept her shoulders hunched showed years of wariness from whatever she'd been put through. Even when Annabelle had first been brought to the bar, she'd had a chip on her shoulder. Annabelle didn't cower to anyone.

She might only be five foot six but Annabelle's attitude was big enough to go up against all the huge shifters who surrounded her.

Maybe one day, Samantha would regain her confidence. If anyone could give Samantha the chance of reclaiming her strength, it was them.

"Can I have some water, please?" Samantha asked.

"You got it," Annabelle said, stepping toward the fridge.

The guys would probably start guzzling coffee when they got there, as they'd need the caffeine to keep them up to make plans. Annabelle hoped she'd be able to get some more sleep, so she chose two bottles of water for herself and Samantha.

As she passed by Kelly, she saw a couple of dishes already

set on the side. Annabelle picked up one with a variety of cheeses, meats, crackers and fruit and carried it over. Samantha's eyes lit up at the food as Annabelle set it in the middle of the table. Annabelle put down the water bottles then picked up a stack of paper plates from the counter.

"Help yourself," Annabelle told her.

She set the plates down before going back and picking up bowls of chips. Kelly flipped hamburger patties on the grill and Annabelle's stomach started to growl. She'd shifted for several hours earlier but hadn't eaten after since it'd been so late. She was really hungry now that she'd smelled the food.

Samantha loaded a plate with a couple of crackers and a small amount of fruit. Annabelle hoped she'd eat more than that. While the dark circles under Samantha's eyes spoke of her being exhausted, Samantha was also very skinny. Like she hadn't had a good meal in a lot longer than the road trip would have taken.

Annabelle really wanted to know Samantha's story but it wasn't her place to ask. Instead, she took the seat next to Samantha and reached for some of the fruit. She didn't fill the silence with small talk. In her experience, Samantha would be thinking about what she'd run from and what was going to happen now. As much as Annabelle wanted to take Samantha's thoughts away, Annabelle knew she needed to take her cues from Samantha.

"I really appreciate all this," Samantha whispered.

"It's what we do," Annabelle replied honestly.

"I'm glad," Samantha said.

Annabelle patted her shoulder, pleased when Samantha leaned in to her touch instead of flinching away. There were many reasons that the underground organization Mac ran even existed. Mac had been taking in strays, like herself, for years.

She'd been fourteen when Mac had come across her living in an alley, sleeping behind a Dumpster. After running away from her twelfth foster home, Annabelle was not going to go back into the system. Mac had offered her an alternative. And it wasn't sick and twisted the way all the other offers she'd gotten had been. Mac had just opened the Den and needed help with the nephew he had custody of. Duffy had been seven when Mac had brought Annabelle home. Now, thirteen years later, this group was the family she loved, the only one she'd ever had.

Mac, Calvin and Duffy walked into the room and Annabelle smiled up at them. Mac was the father figure who'd raised her, made sure she had enough to eat, a place to sleep, love and affection. Duffy was a little brother to her. When Duffy had fallen in love with Calvin, Annabelle had had another brother. The others in the group were like cousins, uncles, aunts and other extended family members. It was all she'd ever wanted. Getting to help shifters in trouble gave her an extra purpose. She felt as if she was making the world a better place.

Calvin ran his fingers across Annabelle's shoulder before he took a seat on the other side of Samantha, with Duffy and Mac sitting across from them. Even if trouble had come home with Calvin and Duffy, she was happy they'd returned.

"Feeling better?" Calvin asked Samantha quietly.

"Yes, thank you," Samantha replied. She looked at Mac. "Thank you for taking me in."

"Of course," Mac said. "We want to help in any way that we can."

Samantha nodded.

"Burgers!" Kelly announced, carrying a platter of meat and buns to the table.

"Oh, God," Calvin moaned. "I missed your cooking."

"Me, too," Duffy agreed, already reaching for the food.

Mac slapped his hand. "Ladies first," he growled. "Didn't I teach you manners?"

Duffy gave Mac a sheepish grin. "Sorry, but if I'd had to eat fast food one more day, I was going to do something drastic, like order a salad."

Everyone laughed, including Samantha, which seemed to be the break in tension that they'd needed. They began to eat. The food disappeared quickly while Annabelle shared looks and smiles with the group. The loneliness that usually surrounded her was absent. At least for a while. Eventually Calvin and Duffy would return to the road, Kelly would be buried in a cookbook, trying to find new recipes, and Mac's job would have him stressed and locked in his office. But, for the moment, her family was with her and that made her content.

By the time their stomachs were full, Samantha's head bobbed in exhaustion.

"Hey." Annabelle laid her palm against Samantha's back. "How about I show you to your room and let you shower and get some sleep?"

"That'd be great," Samantha said.

Annabelle stood, glancing at Mac. He gave her a discreet nod to take Samantha downstairs. They guys would make sure that there was no lingering trace of Samantha, including her scent. Samantha gazed around as they walked through the narrow hallway that led to the bedrooms. Six of their group lived on that level. As far as anyone knew, they were the only ones who resided in the back rooms.

A mist sprayed over their heads and Samantha flinched.

"A scent neutralizer," Annabelle explained. "No one will ever know you were here."

Samantha laughed nervously. "Okay."

"This way," Annabelle said when they reached the end of the corridor. She moved aside a picture of the family to reveal a security panel. Before she punched in the four numbers needed, she glanced over her shoulder at Samantha. "Ready?"

Samantha's eyes were wide, but she nodded in response.

Excitement coursed through Annabelle. She loved going down to the lower level. It looked like an entirely different building. While the bar appeared rundown and barely able to keep standing, that was just the surface appearance. The modern high-tech of the converted basement was amazing.

She tapped in the code and the wood separated, revealing a three-inch-thick steel door. Annabelle stepped forward to run her hands over the shiny barrier until she found the notch where the latch was located. She pulled down and a click sounded before the door unlocked.

"Wow!" Samantha murmured.

"Just wait," Annabelle said.

She had to push the door open, but it moved inward silently and smoothly. As soon as she placed her foot inside, the motion sensor light triggered, illuminating the entry to the underground bunker.

Down here was a whole different world. The walls were solid concrete to keep those who needed to hide safe and out of view. But the homey feel of the space surprised most people.

The barrier opened into a large living area. Black leather couches and chairs were scattered around the room, alongside heavy, dark-wood furniture. Directly across the room was a small kitchen area and off to one side, the office had been set up. Monitors lined the walls, showing feeds from the numerous security cameras around the property. The hum of the computers was the only sound in the quiet space.

"Let me show you where you can sleep," Annabelle said. Samantha remained standing in the doorway. When she moved forward, Annabelle pushed the door closed until she heard the locks reengage. On the other side, the wood panel would be back in place. "There are three bedrooms down here. Someone will be out here in the main room at all times."

"You do this a lot," Samantha commented.

"Yes," Annabelle admitted. There was no reason to lie.

"When Cal and Duffy offered to get me to safety, I had no idea all this existed." She waved her hand around. "I don't... I don't know what to do."

Annabelle took her hand and drew her to the couch. It

sounded as though Samantha needed to talk to someone. They sank into the big comfortable cushions, which was one of the best feelings in the world to Annabelle. "All you have to do relax, trust that we know what we're doing and get some rest. Before you know it, you'll have a brand-new life."

"How can you do all this?" Samantha asked.

It was a common question. "Each one of us has our own reasons for getting involved in this organization. In the beginning, when Mac first set this up as a safe house, we mainly dealt with domestic disputes. Women who needed to get away from an abusive husband or boyfriend. Because of our animal sides, it can be harder for a shifter to escape. Most of us have it bred into us to listen to our Alpha, the dominant, or whatever we have. It's difficult to fight back when that person is the abuser."

"Yeah, it is," Samantha whispered.

Annabelle remained holding Samantha's hand and the fox shifter began to squeeze harder.

"After the humans were told about the existence of shifters, we expanded. Sometimes the laws don't protect us. It's a sad but true fact. We help those who need a new life." Annabelle believed in what they did. She'd seen too many men, women and children come through those doors who'd had no hope until Mac had worked his magic and found them a place where they might regain the life that had been stolen from them.

"You didn't ask me what happened," Samantha whispered.

"Because you don't have to tell me," Annabelle assured her. "If you don't ever want to think about it again, you don't have to. But if you want to talk to someone, I am more than happy to listen. I've been told I'm pretty good at it." She offered what she hoped came off as an encouraging smile.

"I'm pregnant," Samantha said, placing her hand protectively across her stomach.

"Oh!" Annabelle reached over and laid her palm to cover Samantha's. "A baby!"

"If I'd stayed, I would lose this child like I did my first one. He would have beaten me until I miscarried again."

"Your husband?" Annabelle asked gently.

"No," Samantha said. "I wouldn't marry him, but he refused let me go. My brother Mike got money and a high position in our troop. He's the only family I had. He turned his back on me, though. I begged for help, but all my brother cared about was moving up in rank."

"I'm so sorry." Annabelle felt tears gathering.

"I thought, when I got pregnant the first time, the abuse would stop. I honestly believed Frank would be happy about a child. I couldn't have been more wrong. He was furious. Frank wouldn't allow anyone or anything to take my attention from him."

Annabelle had heard similar stories before, but this still sickened and shocked her. "No one helped?" She didn't know why she'd asked. A part of her just wanted to hear that someone had attempted to come to this poor girl's defense.

"No one's going to report a crime the sheriff was responsible for," Samantha said.

Fuck. Annabelle scooted over and tugged Samantha close until the little fox shifter sobbed against her shoulder. Once again, someone was using the law to protect themselves instead of the innocent. In Annabelle's experience, she'd never come across an honest police official. That was why the group did what they did.

She waited until Samantha's crying jag finished before pulling away. "If you could go anywhere in the world, where would it be?" she asked.

Samantha shook her head. "No idea. I just want to live somewhere private where no one will bother me. I want to raise my child in a loving home."

Annabelle grinned. "You'll get that."

"How can you be so sure?"

"Because our network is vast," Annabelle said. "You'll end up right where you're supposed to. I believe that with all my heart."

"I have a hard time trusting any of this. The entire ride here I expected Frank or my brother to come after us," Samantha confessed. "I still expect them to come busting in."

"They won't," Annabelle assured her.

"How can you know that?"

"Others have tried," Annabelle told her. "No one has ever gotten down here. You're safe." Even if the bar was breached, no one would find the entrance to the lower level. They'd run tests and drills, making sure.

Samantha nodded. "If your two friends hadn't come across Frank beating me in a parking lot, I don't know what might have happened."

"How'd they get you out of there?"

"Calvin jumped in and saved me. He kept punching Frank until Frank fell to the ground. The restaurant was closed and none of the troop was there because we weren't even supposed to be out of our territory. I'd run off because I found out I'm pregnant and Frank didn't want the others to know that I'd taken off on him again. Duffy stepped in front of me, sort of guarding me, in case Frank got up."

"Sound like our guys," Annabelle commented.

"I wish he'd killed Frank," Samantha whispered the admission.

"I understand." Annabelle meant it, too.

"Instead, once Frank was unconscious, Calvin turned to me and said, 'If you want to leave here, we have somewhere safe we can take you. If not, we'll leave you alone. It's your choice, but you have to make it now.' So I chose to go with them."

"I'm glad you did."

"Me, too," Samantha replied. "I think I'd like to shower now."

"Good," Annabelle said. She rose, pulling Samantha up

with her.

The first room was the largest and also had the biggest bathroom, so Annabelle led Samantha in that direction. *Samantha deserves some pampering.*

"Here," Annabelle said, pushing open the bedroom door. The décor was soft blues that she had read somewhere would give the space a relaxing atmosphere. Mac had allowed Annabelle to fix up the rooms. She hoped the people who stayed there found them peaceful.

"It's beautiful," Samantha praised.

"There are clean clothes in the dresser. We have all different sizes, so take whatever you want," Annabelle said. "The bathroom is stocked with everything you should need."

Samantha turned to her. "Thank you."

"You're very welcome," Annabelle pulled her into a quick hug before stepping out and closing the door behind her.

Trent and Carter would return at any minute, so they'd probably head down there. Carter took care of the group's IT needs. He'd no doubt be watching the cameras for the next several hours. Annabelle walked toward the little kitchen area with its fridge, microwave, stove and small pantry. Kelly was really good at keeping it stocked so that if they had emergency cases like Samantha, the group was prepared.

Annabelle started a pot of coffee before walking to the couch. She picked up the blanket off the back and wrapped it around herself, then lay her head against the arm. She was really tired.

She heard the water turn on in Samantha's room. The rooms down there weren't soundproofed, because part of watching over their charges meant whoever was on guard duty needed to hear what happened inside the other rooms. Sometimes the people who came to them for help became so overwhelmed that they tried to harm themselves.

Not hearing anything to worry about, Annabelle closed her eyes.

The adrenaline from earlier was slowly leaving, making her body feel heavy. It had been a couple of months since they'd had anyone needing their help. Sometimes it happened like that. They'd go for a while without any guests, or sometimes they'd be spread thin by having more than one person who needed assistance.

During the times when it was just her small family around, they played in their shifted forms and worked the bar. The residents in Brookside were all shifters. No humans stayed longer than a few nights. It was the town secret, so that when humans showed up, the population of the small quiet town didn't do anything to draw attention to their differences. It was a shifter's choice whether he or she decided to be out in public or not. The inhabitants of Brookside all kept their shifter ability secret. It allowed them to remain safe.

The locks disengaging caught her attention and she opened her eyes. Carter walked in first with Trent right behind him, which didn't surprise her. She hadn't been expecting Mac, Calvin or Duffy, though. Mac cocked his head, no doubt listening to where Samantha had gotten off to, and nodded.

"She's showering? Good. That should help her relax. How's she doing?" Mac asked, striding toward where Annabelle sat.

"Yes," Annabelle said. They'd have a few minutes to talk without Samantha hearing them. "I think she's doing okay. A little scared about what's going to happen but grateful that she got away."

"It was lucky we came across her," Calvin commented. He sat in the chair next to the couch.

"You're her hero," Annabelle teased.

Calvin just shook his head.

"You should have seen him," Duffy said, dropping down beside her on the couch. He pulled her legs onto her lap to rub the soles of her feet. "He was a total badass."

"Which you need to be careful about," Mac told Calvin. "You could have gotten yourself arrested or worse."

"I know, boss. I saw him hit her and lost it. Samantha was so much smaller than this guy. He was at least six foot two and two hundred and eight pounds."

"Damn," Annabelle said. "She can't be more than five two and I'd be surprised if she weighed more than one ten."

"Yeah," Calvin said. He looked at Mac. "I know I messed up. We tried to cover our tracks, but I don't know if we got away clean. He's a fucking sheriff. I'm sorry."

"It's okay." Mac grasped Calvin's shoulder, giving him a firm squeeze. Annabelle watched as Mac turned fatherly. "We can handle it. The important thing is you brought that girl here and you and Duffy are safe."

"I'll make up for it," Calvin promised.

"Cal," Mac said, moving to crouch in front of him. "There's nothing to make up for. Yes, you made some mistakes, but I'm proud of you. If someone had stepped in when the same thing was happening with my sister, she'd still be here."

Duffy's hand tightened on her foot. It wasn't often that Mac brought up Charlotte's murder. A sweet girl killed by her jealous husband who'd been abusing her for years. Mac had still been in the army and hadn't seen Charlotte much, and he'd had no idea what she'd been dealing with. Not until he'd gotten the call that she was dead, killed by her husband, before he'd turned the gun on himself. Duffy had been found hiding in his closet, a scared and traumatized boy.

"Mac," Calvin whispered.

"I hope this fucker does come here," Mac said, menacingly pounding a fist into the palm of his other hand. "We'll show him what's it's like to fight someone his own size."

Calvin nodded. "Okay."

"Why don't you two go get cleaned up and some sleep? Trent and Carter are on the cameras," Mac said.

"Yeah." Calvin ran his hands roughly over his face.

Duffy patted her leg before rising.

Annabelle waited until Calvin and Duffy had left, the door closing behind them, to peer up at Mac. "You okay?"

She glanced into the office area, but Trent and Carter were busy on the computers.

Mac sighed deeply and dropped down into the chair that Calvin had sat in earlier. "I have a really bad feeling about this."

"What? Why?" She straightened up.

"I don't know," Mac said. "I just feel like this isn't going to be a simple case."

"We'll be okay, though, right? We'll get Samantha out of here?"

"Oh you can count on that." Mac leaned forward, dropping his hands between his knees. "I'll never let anyone hurt any of you. We have to move fast and cover our tracks, but Samantha is going to be safe. She and the baby will have a good life."

Annabelle bit her lip. Now she was scared. If Mac had any concern about Samantha's situation, then Annabelle needed to consider what might happen. If any strangers showed up she'd keep her eye on them. No one was going to threaten what they were doing there.

* * * *

Logan Coldwell was ready for the day to be done with. He'd spent the morning testifying in court on an old case before he'd returned to his office to finish some paperwork. His partner of two years, Olivia, was off on personal leave to take care of her father, who'd suffered a heart attack, and Logan missed her. He didn't have a lot of friends and wasn't close to anyone other than his partner inside the Coalition.

It was already after the end of his shift so he didn't know why he still sat in his office, when all he really wanted to do was go home and have a beer or two. Yeah, he did — he just didn't want to go to his lonely apartment. Still, he couldn't spend his evening there. Logan glanced across the room at the mirror on the wall. He needed to move the fucking thing. Every time he caught a glimpse of himself Logan saw how old he was beginning to look.

Instead of his neatly cut dark-blond hair Logan saw the gray hairs that were starting to come in. His pale blue eyes had such dark circles under them it appeared he'd aged ten years in the last three. If he didn't start taking better care of himself he wasn't going to recognize himself soon. He still spent plenty of time at the gym, making sure he remained in top shape to work in the field, but stress and loneliness took their toll.

Logan stood and yanked his suit jacket off his chair, and his desk phone rang. He shook his head. It figured that the second he decided to go home, he'd get a fucking call.

"Agent Coldwell," he said while slinging his jacket into the guest chair before taking a seat again.

"Hey, Logan, it's Jamie Ward."

"Jamie!" Logan exclaimed. It had been a long time since he'd spoken to his fellow Coalition agent. They both worked for the government agency that had been formed after the announcement of shifters to the world. The Coalition's purpose was to protect innocent shifters while at the same time dealing with those who broke the laws.

"Hey, man," Jamie said. "It's good to talk to you. How long has it been?"

"At least a year," Logan replied. "I heard you fell in love and settled down."

Jamie's laugh was boisterous. "Yes. Her name is Brandy and she's amazing."

"That's great, man," Logan told him. He'd met Jamie when they'd both attended the police academy in Phoenix. Back then, they'd had to keep their abilities a secret, so they'd bonded. Late at night, they'd sneak out to shift into their animals. It had been weird for Logan to transform with a bear, since he'd always gone through the change alone.

"I'd love for you to meet her," Jamie said. "You haven't been back to Arizona since we graduated from the academy."

There were reasons for that, but Logan didn't want

to think about them. "No, I haven't. This is the smallest division of the Coalition, but I like it here." It wasn't a lie either. Logan wouldn't be happy in a large office like Jamie worked in.

"Good," Jamie said. "I'm glad you're happy. But, hey, I need some help from your neck of the woods."

Logan chuckled. "Sure, man, what's up?"

"I got a missing person report from the head of a fox troop about thirty minutes from here," Jamie explained. "The guy's sheriff in a town called Baylor. His girlfriend was taken after two men attacked him."

"Shifters or human?" Even if the sheriff was a fox, he would be stronger than any human.

"Shifters. Some kind of large cat. He wasn't sure what species the other guy was, though. Something as strong, he guesses."

"Ah," Logan said.

The feline species remained one of the largest and it was difficult to tell the different types apart if someone wasn't used to their scents.

"He got the license plates of the men's motorcycles and passed them along to me. I'm sure he did his own search as well. The address registered to the suspects is located about an hour from you. The place is called Brookside."

"Doesn't sound familiar," Logan said. "But if you send me the details, I'll check it out. I can even drive out there tonight if you want."

"That'd be great." Jamie sounded relieved. "I can't get away right now. I'm working a case of a woman who took her two kids from her shifter husband and disappeared."

Logan growled. "She human?"

"Yeah, and I want to get those boys back to their dad."

"Email me everything you have and I'll take this off your hands. I'm closer and if we're dealing with the felines, I'll probably have better luck getting close."

"That's what I'm hoping," Jamie admitted. "I'm sending you my report now."

Logan moved his mouse to his email and clicked it open so he'd see when the file arrived. "I'm still at the office. I'll call you after I know something."

"Thanks, man. I really appreciate this."

"It's not a problem," Logan assured him. "I'm happy to help."

"There's just one more thing."

"What's wrong?" A chill went through Logan as Jamie dropped his voice and spoke seriously.

"Something's not right with this sheriff's story," Jamie told him. "Or maybe just off about him. I added the search I did on him as well. I don't trust this guy at all, so be careful."

Logan was grateful for the warning. Jamie had the best instincts of anyone Logan had ever met. If Jamie said something was wrong with the sheriff, then Logan would be wise to listen. "I'll be careful."

"If you run into any trouble, let me know. I can send one of the other team leaders if I need to."

"I'll keep you informed, but I have a pretty good group that I work with here," Logan said. "They'll back me up if I need it."

The *ding* of an incoming message sounded. "I got your email. Let me look this over."

"Sure," Jamie said. "And thanks again for helping out."

"I'll talk to you soon," Logan replied, distracted. He was already clicking the attachment open.

"Later."

Logan held the phone for several moments after Jamie had hung up. It appeared that Jamie had only gotten the call from the sheriff five hours ago, and already the Intel that he'd gathered was impressive. The dial tone blaring from the phone surprised him and he laid the instrument in the cradle.

"Let's see what we have," Logan murmured.

The first page was the report Sheriff Frank Nunez had made. Logan read through it twice before moving on. All the answers the sheriff had given were what they should be — perfect. *Too perfect.*

Samantha Jones was a pretty young woman who didn't work and had been living with Frank for five years. She had one sibling who did construction but with whom she didn't seem close. Jamie had tried to locate some of Samantha's friends to speak with in case they knew something about her disappearance, but he hadn't been able to find any.

A feeling of dread filled Logan.

Staring at the driver's license photo of Samantha Jones, Logan saw a sad woman who had a look of defeat in her eyes. Logan wanted to find her. Not to reunite her with the boyfriend, but to make sure she was all right.

The sheriff had called in a kidnapping, but Logan had to wonder if the guy, Frank, hadn't done something to harm Samantha. It wouldn't be the first time that a killer had called in, saying their spouse was missing.

That led to the two men who Sheriff Nunez was fingering for the crime.

Logan clicked through the pages until he got to the two suspects' information.

Calvin Montgomery and Douglas Gordon. They had the same address in Brookside, California. Logan opened his Internet browser and typed in the address. He expected a residence and was surprised when it pulled up a bar called the Den, owned by one Mackenzie Gordon. *Has to be a relative of Douglas.*

He printed out directions to the bar before returning to the email attachment. Jamie had also requested several cameras' feeds from the route home the two bikers would have taken from where they'd snatched Samantha. The feeds hadn't come through yet, but they would help Logan in his investigation. He'd at least see if Samantha had left with the two men or if the sheriff was full of shit. In the meantime, he'd do a little poking around where Calvin and Douglas lived. Logan printed out the entire file Jamie had sent, to put in a binder.

It looked like he was going for a drink.

Chapter Two

Logan pulled his Dodge truck up in front of the bar and shut off his headlights, letting the vehicle idle as he stared at the front of the Den. It didn't look like much. Logan didn't know what he'd actually expected, but the rundown wood building wasn't it.

During the drive, he'd had his computer running searches on the two shifters who were his suspects, plus anyone with a known connection to them. There wasn't much information about Calvin Montgomery — only that he'd grown up in Wyoming and graduated from high school there. He'd then moved moving on. He'd worked various types of labor jobs before finally settling in Brookside.

Douglas 'Duffy' Gordon owned a tattoo shop in Brookside, although his home address was the bar. His mother had been killed several years ago by his father and he'd gone to live with an uncle.

Neither man had any criminal record, so Logan wasn't sure how'd they gotten mixed up with a fox troop.

The other name that had popped up in his research was that of Mackenzie Gordon. Mackenzie had served twelve years in the US Army before buying property in Brookside. He owned the land the bar sat on, along with Duffy's tattoo shop, plus a couple of other buildings. He'd made a life for himself and his nephew. Logan admired what Mackenzie had accomplished. But he had to push that aside and find a missing girl.

He'd pulled over right before he'd reached the town population sign and changed clothes. Luckily, since he did quite a bit of driving and he never knew when he'd be called out to an investigation, Logan kept a packed bag in his trunk. He'd figured he'd get a warmer welcome in jeans and a T-shirt than his suit.

Logan turned off the engine then opened the door and climbed out.

The first thing that caught his attention was the abundant mixture of shifter scents. Several different species.

A chill raced up his spine. It was not common for shifters to congregate together. Too many dominant urges and fearful responses. The predators and the prey. Logan picked up the scent of both here.

This was a very interesting town.

He strode to the door with long, sure strides. He was one of the most powerful shifters in the world. He was also a trained agent of the Shifter Coalition, and he had a mission.

There was no one hanging around, so he pulled open the wide door, preparing himself for anything. Stepping inside, Logan relaxed immediately. There was no threat waiting to jump out at him. Instead, he walked inside a regular-looking bar. Music played quietly from a jukebox in the corner. The décor was mostly rock-and-roll memorabilia and neon beer manufacturer signs.

A few people glanced up at him then returned to what they'd been doing before he'd entered. No one appeared to care much about him.

Two coyotes, bobcat, bird of some kind... He noted all the different species of shifters quickly. There was even a human drinking a dark ale. *Unbelievable.* Logan stalked toward the bar, where a breathtaking black-haired beauty was cleaning glasses. She glanced up at him, giving him a long once-over, and smiled.

"What can I get you?" she asked.

There'd been interest in her gaze. A slow curl of arousal spiraled down his spine to settle into his balls. What a lovely find here in the middle of nowhere. He gave her his best grin. "Whatever you have on tap," he replied, taking a seat on one of the stools. He breathed deeply. *Feline.* Good, but there was a tint of something he couldn't place. An unusual aroma of…bark? He didn't know what he picked up.

"You got it," she said.

When she turned around and bent to grab a cold pilsner from a cooler, he couldn't resist checking out her ass. It was a very nice ass. She poured the gold liquid from the tap for him with expertise.

Before he got distracted by his cock or curiosity about her animal, he angled himself so he could look around the room. The bar wasn't big, with only half a dozen men drinking. He didn't spot the men he was looking for.

"Here you go." The bartender slid his beer in front of him. "Get you anything else?"

"You sell food here?" He probably should have stopped on the road and picked up some fast food, but he hated eating and driving. Actually, he hated having any kind of food in his truck. He'd grown up in filth and would never live that way again.

"Sure do." She reached under the counter and pulled out a laminated menu. "My name's Annabelle. Just holler whenever you're ready to order."

"Thanks." She really was quite pretty, with her long dark hair cascading down her back, and bright, expressive green eyes. Her makeup was heavy around her eyes, but the flawless skin seemed natural. Annabelle was probably in her mid-twenties, which put her at least five years younger than him. He considered making a play for her, but he needed to concentrate on the job first. There would be time later.

She nodded, picking up a coffee pot then walking out from behind the bar. A large man with a full beard and a sharp gaze sat at a table in the corner with an unopened book in front of him. Logan hadn't even noticed the biker, which made him uneasy. Years of training had taught him to be aware of his surroundings, to know when a threat was near, and he'd somehow missed the biggest danger in the room.

Logan swiveled around to face the bar but kept his eyes on the mirror behind the bottles. He could track Annabelle's movements as she stopped by several tables, saying a few words while making her way to the lone guy.

The man watched Logan, though. Their gazes met in the mirror. Logan sat still, waiting. If there was going to be trouble, then it would be with this guy.

Annabelle reached the table and poured coffee into a white ceramic mug. The biker said something to her, causing her to lean down to hear him better. Logan ignored the glimpse of her breasts from her low-cut top. Or at least, he tried to. Sitting with an erection was not comfortable, but he had bigger worries at the moment.

Her gaze shifted to him before she nodded and straightened.

Logan wasn't surprised when she walked directly behind the bar. She set the coffee pot back and turn to him.

"Did you decide?" she asked.

That wasn't what he expected her to say. Caught off guard, he simply nodded. He hadn't actually even looked at the menu, so he glanced down quickly.

"Can I get a bacon cheeseburger with everything and fries?" he requested.

"Sure." She took the menu from him, replacing it under the counter. "I'll put your order in. If you want to take your beer over," she nodded in the direction of the biker, "Mac would like to speak to you."

"Mac?" he questioned.

"He owns the place," she said as she left him. Her demeanor had changed. She no longer looked at him with interest, but instead concern filled her gaze.

Ah, Mackenzie Gordon. The photo Logan had seen was an old one, from when Mac had still been in the service. Mackenzie was almost unrecognizable now.

Logan picked up his glass then slid off the stool. He kept his gaze on Mac's as he sauntered across the room. Mac lifted his head and nodded toward the seat opposite him.

"Have a seat, Agent."

It took all his control not to flinch in surprise. Instead he pulled out the chair and sat. "Good evening."

"Well, it was," Mac said. "Until a member of the Coalition showed up in my bar." Mac leaned forward and his gaze hardened. "What's the Coalition want here?"

Suspicious fucker. Logan liked that. "Can't a guy stop in for a beer?"

"The closest office is over an hour from here," Mac said. "Try again."

Logan leaned back and crossed his arms over his chest. "How'd you know?"

"I have my ways," Mac replied.

Logan snorted. "Really? That's what you're going with?"

"It's my job to protect the shifters in this town," Mac told him. "I take that responsibility seriously."

"Quite a bit of responsibility," Logan stated in disbelief. "For one man." He sniffed. "Even if you are a bear."

Mac didn't appear impressed. "I have help," he admitted. "A pack of sorts."

"Your bartender is feline and the woman in the kitchen some sort of bird. I've also picked up hyena, deer and wolf strongly. They're here a lot."

"Yes, and it works," Mac said. "Without any interference from the Coalition."

Okay, so Mac had issues with authority. Logan wasn't really that surprised. "I'm not here to cause you any problems."

This time Mac snorted. "You just *being* here is a problem. So I'll ask you again, what do you want?"

He was disappointed but wouldn't let it show. The place was so interesting and he wanted to learn more about it and its occupants, especially the pretty little waitress.

Logan leaned forward to pull his cellphone out of his back pocket. He scrolled through his email until he got to the picture of Samantha Jones, then slid the device across the table.

Mac reached down and picked it up.

"Have you seen her?" Logan questioned.

"No," Mac replied, looking him in the eye.

Logan didn't detect any dishonesty. When someone lied, it was easy to tell. Their body gave off signs. Mac's heartbeat hadn't changed, he wasn't sweating and there was no change of pitch in his voice. Still, Logan knew Mac was hiding something. He just didn't know what or why.

"Bacon cheeseburger and fries," Annabelle said, coming up behind him.

"Thank you," he told her, leaning back so she could set his plate down. Before she left, he reached and snagged his cell back from Mac. "Have you seen this woman?"

Annabelle took the phone from him, brushing her fingers against his. Her eyes widened at the touch and she actually shivered. *Damn.* He bit down a growl. He didn't know what kind of feline she was, but the lion inside him wanted to see her submit to him. Logan licked his lips, leaning forward. Annabelle stared at him in surprise. Oh yeah, he liked the way she eyed him.

"Ah-hem." Mac cleared his throat and Annabelle recoiled from him.

Logan glared at the bear shifter and tapped the photo on his cell. "Have you ever seen her before?"

Annabelle glanced down and frowned. "No, should I have?"

"I guess not," Logan said, retrieving his phone. Again, he didn't detect any dishonesty. She didn't look away from him, didn't glance toward Mac. So why did Logan still feel that they had been prepared for him? Like they'd expected to see him. There hadn't been any surprise on Mac's part.

"I'll get you another beer," Annabelle said, hurrying off with a faint blush to her cheeks.

"That was interesting," Mac commented.

Logan watched Annabelle until she was behind the bar before he turned his attention back to Mac. "Is this where you warn me away from her?"

"I won't have to," Mac said. "She doesn't know who you are, but when she learns, you won't stand a chance." He rose then. "Enjoy your meal."

Mac strode across the room, heading toward the kitchen. Logan really wanted to follow him and demand more answers. To see where he went. *What are these people hiding?* Instead, he pulled his plate closer to him. Mac might have left, but that did give Logan full access to the woman.

"Do you need anything else?" Annabelle asked, setting his fresh beer down.

"Some answers," Logan requested.

"Answers?" she repeated slowly.

"How long have you worked here?"

Annabelle's head snapped up. "What?"

"I believe you heard the question." He was growing tired of this game. Yes, he was an agent, but he was also a powerful shifter. Respect, especially from another feline, should be given. It took all his control not to order Annabelle to do his bidding. It was hard, but he did manage to push down the instinct. He wasn't a bully. He might have grown up around assholes who abused their power, but he wasn't like them. He'd joined the Coalition to prove himself better than them. He relaxed his shoulders and tried to smile. He'd been too harsh, he knew, but before he managed to apologize, she spoke.

"Why are you asking me that?" She took a step back. "Who are you?"

Annabelle deserved to know why he was there, too. *Guess I'll find out if what Mac said is true.* He pulled out his wallet and flipped it open, revealing his badge. "Agent Logan Coldwell, Shifter Coalition."

She paled while jumping away. "A cop?"

"An agent, actually," he corrected gently. "And I'm looking for the woman I showed you a picture of earlier. Are you sure you haven't seen her?"

"I haven't," she said quietly. "She's very pretty. I'm sure if she came in here, I would remember."

"Did you work last night?" he questioned.

"Yes," she said. "And she didn't come in."

"What about Calvin Montgomery or Douglas Gordon? Did they come in?"

He'd hoped to catch her off guard. She tilted her head and the frown returned. "No. I closed up at two and went to bed half an hour later. They didn't come in while I was on shift."

"You live close by?"

"I live here," she answered.

"Here? At the bar?"

"There's living quarters in the rear. Yes, I live here in the bar," she said.

"And your relationship to Mac?" he asked. It was more of a personal question than professional, but he'd wrap it up in business.

"How's that any of your concern? Why are you asking about Cal and Duffy?"

Logan shook his head. "Everything is part of Coalition business."

The change took over immediately. Her bright-green eyes dimmed while she clenched her jaw. "No, it's not. We're none of your concern. So why don't you finish your dinner and move along? Or I could pack it up for you to take with you."

She whirled on her heel and stomped toward the bar.

He'd obviously worn out his welcome. Which was a shame, since it was the best first bite he'd ever had. The flavor of the meat burst on his tongue and he took another bite before he'd even swallowed the first.

As he shoveled food down his throat, he kept an eye on his surroundings. No one else had entered the bar, but at least one table had cleared out. Mac hadn't shown back up, but now that Logan knew the place had living quarters, he didn't expect to see the other man again. He hadn't spotted Calvin or Douglas, but he needed to return to his office and regroup before he came back and asked about them.

Logan had the feeling that he'd stumbled onto something more than just a missing woman. There was no scent or sign of a fox shifter, so if they did have her, they weren't holding her at the bar. He'd drive by the tattoo shop and the other locations Mac owned before heading out of town.

He took a long drink of his beer, eyeing Annabelle. Whether or not they wanted him to, Logan would be returning soon.

Annabelle held it together until the Coalition agent left the bar. She went to the window and watched as he climbed into a dark-blue Dodge truck and drove away. Out of habit, she memorized his license plate number.

Once the agent — Logan, he'd said his name was — had pulled out of the parking lot, she spun on her heel and stalked toward Mac's room. Kelly started to stay something as Annabelle strode through the kitchen, but she held up a hand to stop her.

She passed by the other closed doors until she reached Mac's. Annabelle burst into the room.

Mac glanced up from the book he'd been reading on his bed. "Is he gone?"

"A Coalition agent?" she shrieked. "What are we going to do?"

"Relax." Mac tossed his book to the end of the bed. "He doesn't know anything."

"He asked questions!"

"Hey! Come here." Mac caught her hand and drew her down next to him.

"They might find her," Annabelle said. This was all getting messed up. They'd always guaranteed safety and protection. They had never failed.

Mac had worked all night to find a place for Samantha and in planning for Calvin and Duffy to get back on the road.

Samantha had been extremely thankful as Calvin and Duffy had loaded up one of the SUVs to drive her to

Missouri. She'd never been away from the west coast. The area that Samantha would be settled in had beautiful green fields in the summer and got snow in the winter. The farmhouse where she would live needed some fixing up, but she'd even been excited about that. Annabelle wanted Samantha to raise her baby in that wonderful environment.

"What if he knows I lied?" she asked.

They'd never had this kind of trouble before. Sure, the cops had sniffed around and asked questions, but never had the Coalition gotten involved.

"It's going to be okay," Mac assured her, rubbing her back as she leaned against him. "Have I ever let anyone hurt you?"

"It's not me I'm worried about," she told him.

"You really connected with Samantha, didn't you?"

"Yes," she admitted. "She's already lost one baby, but she's determined to give the one she's carrying a great life. When I spoke to her this morning, she really believed she was getting a fresh start. I don't want the Coalition to take that away from her."

"They won't," Mac said. "This agent is here because of Samantha's ex. He's a sheriff and using his authority to try and intimidate us. He could have come after us, but instead he's using the Coalition."

"Do you think it's over?" *Please, please let us not have to worry about the Coalition.*

"No, honey," Mac said. "But I don't think this agent even knows what he's searching for. He thinks that we took Samantha against her will. We'll let him poke around and he won't find anything."

"What about Cal and Duffy?" she asked.

They were her brothers and if they were going to get in trouble, she had to do something to help them.

"They'll be fine," Mac said. "There's no proof that they did anything other than give her a ride. There's no evidence."

She nodded. This wasn't the first time they'd had to go up against opposition, but normally it was the abusive spouse, the human hunter or someone like that. She was scared of the Coalition. They had the resources to stop Mac's underground network.

"Do you want to talk about the other thing bothering you?"

She stiffened. Annabelle wasn't going to deny what she was trying to push down.

"Look at me," he urged, gently grasping her chin and lifting her face.

"I'm so sorry!"

"You have nothing to apologize for," he said.

She shook her head. "I was attracted to him." Annabelle whispered the confession even though no one else was close enough to hear. Her face heated and she lowered her head in shame.

Mac chuckled. "There's nothing wrong with that."

"Sure," she said and snorted in disbelief.

"He's a very good-looking man. Dominant and confident. Just the way you like them."

Annabelle frowned. "A little too clean-cut."

"Really?" Mac teased. "Because the way your heartbeat quickened, I—"

"Okay." She held up her hand. "I don't want to talk about it."

"I think we should, though."

"Why?" She didn't understand why Mac was pressing her. "It's not like I'd actually get involved with a Coalition agent. That goes against everything we do."

"Does it?"

He sounded so serious that she had to glance up at him. Why was he confusing the issue?

"If he found out what we do here..." She shuddered just thinking about the implications.

Mac had spent his entire life protecting those who needed it.

"You're going to have to open up to someone at some time. Your reaction to this Agent Coldwell was the most intense and instant I've seen from you. That's not something you can just dismiss."

"You're reading too much into a few minutes with a stranger," Annabelle accused. Her words sounded false even to her own ears, but she had to ignore that. "And I've been attracted to plenty of men before."

"No," Mac said. "You hook up with guys who you consider safe. Ones who'll be gone in a few weeks. I don't think you've ever felt any real connection with any of them."

"Ugh," she muttered. "You make me sound like a slut."

Mac laughed. "Since we both know you've slept with less than a handful of men, that's not true. And I'm not even talking about sex. I'm talking about a connection."

"You're talking nonsense," she told him. Annabelle stood before staring down at him. "But you did take away my worry, so I'll let you get away with it this time."

"Where you going?" Mac rose as well.

"To protect my family."

He caught her hand when she turned around. "How?"

Annabelle smiled at the concern in his voice. "I'm going to learn everything I can about the enemy."

Mac grinned, probably since he'd taught her that. "Okay."

She kissed his cheek and headed for the door, which still stood open.

"I'll watch the bar," Mac said.

"I'm sure Kelly is keeping an eye out," she said. "She saw me headed back here."

"Go downstairs," Mac ordered. "I know you're dying to get started."

She really was. Now that she had a plan, Annabelle might forget all about her damn attraction to the Coalition agent and ensure Samantha's safety. "Thanks."

As she jogged down the hall toward the hidden door, she heard Mac's laughter. It didn't matter, though. She wasn't going to sit idly while a threat loomed against them. Too much work had gone into the underground network they'd set up.

While disengaging the locks to the hidden area, she thought of all the shifters who'd come through here. At fourteen, she hadn't actually understood, but as she'd grown up, Mac had involved her more and more in the group. She was now his number two and he didn't keep secrets from her. She gave him the same respect. He was the father that she'd never had and the guardian she'd needed. Mac had cared about what happened to her. Had taught her, Duffy and all the others that they could make a difference. That it was okay to lean on one another.

That hadn't been easy for Annabelle. While she'd connected with the seven-year-old Duffy, she'd been wary of the rest. Mac had stayed just close enough to offer support, but at the same time, giving her plenty of space. It was a balance that Annabelle still hadn't managed. Slowly, the others who'd hung around the edges had become the family that she now had.

She needed to get control and this was a way she would be able to do that.

Once through the security door, Annabelle strode toward Carter. He was working on a laptop, the piece of equipment in several parts. She glanced at the pink top.

"Is that mine?"

Carter jumped before looking at her with a guilty face. "I'm fixing it."

She knew her mouth hung open, but *shit*. "It wasn't broken."

"I'm making it better." He sniffed and pushed his black-rimmed glasses up his nose.

She growled, snatching a pen and notepad off the desk. "I need you to do something for me."

Carter perked up. "Cool. What is it?"

Annabelle wrote down Logan's name and license plate number. "I need everything, and I mean everything, on this guy." She tore off the piece of paper and handed it to him.

"Okay." He took it from her then turned to his own

computer. He typed fast. She could barely keep up with the movement as his fingers flew over the keyboard.

She knew better to rush him, although it was killing her to pace the room behind him. If she spoke to Carter, he'd snap at her, so she chewed on her lip instead.

"*Fuck!*"

Carter's curse had her leaping to his side. "What?"

"A Coalition agent?"

"Yes," she said. "He was at the bar earlier asking questions and we need to know everything there is to find."

"Are you sure?" Carter asked, cracking his knuckles. It was a nervous tic and she gripped his shoulder.

"You don't have to," she said. "I don't want you getting into trouble."

"It's not like I'll get caught," Carter told her. "I just haven't ever tried getting information on a Coalition agent. The FBI, CIA and local cops, yes, but never the Coalition."

"Maybe this is a bad idea," she murmured. Annabelle didn't like the doubt that formed and grew. Even if Logan was coming for them, that didn't mean she should let Carter get into trouble.

Carter snorted. "Too late. I'm doing this."

"Are you sure?" She sat on the edge of the desk.

"He was here? In our home?"

Annabelle nodded.

"Then I'll get the Intel you want. I just need one thing."

"Sure. What?"

"Leave," he ordered.

"I'm sorry?" She couldn't have heard him right.

"This is going to be some delicate hacking. I don't need you hovering over my shoulder."

"I don't hover," she defended.

"You do. All of you do," Carter said. "Go order me something to eat and bring it to me when it's ready. That should keep you out of my hair for a while."

"You're getting bossy," she complained.

"Food!" he demanded with a grin.

"Fine." She bussed a kiss on his cheek before walking toward the door. "But you better watch it. Anyone else might take a bite out of you."

"Yeah." Carter waved a hand but he'd already bent over his keyboard.

She knew she'd lost him. Nothing that was said would penetrate through Carter's busy brain. He'd gone into work mode.

Annabelle climbed the stairs then let herself out of the security door. Once the barrier closed behind her back, she stilled, listening to make sure that everything was still okay on the main floor.

She heard Kelly humming in the kitchen. Annabelle headed for her friend so she could get Carter's food ordered. She didn't think that Kelly was cooking, instead leaving the job to the full-time employee, Micah. But if the owl shifter knew it was Carter wanting to eat, she'd probably demand to make it.

"Hey," Annabelle said, entering the kitchen. Just as she suspected. Kelly sat on a bar stool as Micah flipped burgers on the grill.

"Are you okay?" Kelly asked as Annabelle stopped beside her. "Mac told me about the agent."

"Yeah," Samantha said. "I put Carter on it. He sent me down here for food."

Her friend jumped off the stool. "I have a new vegetarian recipe I've wanted to try. You can help chop."

"Oh, I was going to…" She waved toward the bar.

"Nope," Kelly said, pushing her in the direction of the sink. "Wash your hands. Mac said he'd take care of the front of the house and I'm guessing Carter kicked you out of the basement, so you get to help me."

Annabelle grumbled but complied before taking a seat on a stool and accepting the cutting board and knife Kelly handed her. While she managed to warm up food and actually made pretty good eggs, she tried to stay out of the kitchen as much as possible.

She didn't want to help right then either, but she also didn't have much of a choice. Everyone else was busy and she needed to keep her mind occupied so she didn't start thinking about the sexy agent from earlier.

There was only so much she could do until Carter got her the Intel she needed.

Chapter Three

Logan hunched over his laptop with a headache pulsing behind his eyes. After leaving the bar the night before he'd driven around the town of Brookside, familiarizing himself with the area.

There'd been few residents on the streets, but the ones he'd seen had looked at him suspiciously. Logan didn't know what was going on, but now he knew he had to get answers.

Before bed, he'd programmed several searches to run. Now, as he sipped his first cup of coffee, he scrolled through the results. He ignored the files that he should be reading for the attachment he needed to see.

Toward the bottom he finally saw it. *Annabelle Sanchez.*

He stared at the name.

His dreams had been filled with her beautiful face. The way she'd looked him up and down with interest. He'd wanted to lay claim to her right then and there. The animal part of him had been at the surface, stretching and yowling to get close to her. The faint scent of her cat had only teased his senses as well. Logan had no idea what species she was, and that was very interesting. Part of his extra training was to recognize the numerous types of felines.

If he opened the attachment, he might just find out all Annabelle's secrets. So why did he hesitate? He wanted to know more about her, but...this felt like cheating. Logan scoffed at himself. This was ridiculous. He wasn't even going to discover everything he needed to know about Annabelle. The Coalition didn't keep Intel on every shifter, but they did have access to all government databases as well as connecting family and community ties. Logan had to be careful with what he used during his legal documenting of cases, because he had access to far greater resources than any of his fellow agents knew about.

He shook his head to dislodge the thoughts about the *other* work he'd done. There were reasons he hadn't visited Arizona, and the secrets he had to keep made him feel even further away from his other agents. He couldn't think about all that, though. It had been months since he'd received a call to do dirty work, but the call was always right around the corner. He'd done things in his life that left him with an overwhelming feeling of disgust. No matter how many shifters he tried to save, he'd never get his soul cleaned. Logan was tarnished, dirty, and would never be worthy of the love he saw others share.

No, his past remained shadowed and he couldn't claim to have changed his ways, since he didn't know what the future contained. There was so much more that Logan might possibly be called on to do.

The ringing of his cell drew him out of his musing.

Logan picked up his phone and saw it was Jamie calling. He hadn't been expecting to talk to the other shifter so soon. Something must have happened.

"Hello."

"Logan," Jamie said. "I hope I'm not interrupting anything?"

"No, I was just going through some searches I started last night."

"The case I gave you?"

"Yeah," Logan said. "I went to the bar and nosed around. The town is something I haven't seen before."

"That's why I'm calling," Jamie said. "One of the other team leaders had some information on it. Zak did some undercover work around that area a few years ago."

Logan had met the tiger shifter a few times, since he was good friends with Jamie, but it was hard for him to be around another large cat who was so dominant. "Why'd he tell you?"

"He'd met Mac Gordon during his assignment and Mac saved his life. Zak says that Mac's solid and if he's involved in the case, then there's a good reason."

Logan thought about everything he'd seen last night. He'd had a feeling that Mac knew more than he'd been admitting, but he'd also known in his gut that the bear shifter wasn't involved in a kidnapping. "I would agree, but there's something going on in that bar. Probably with the entire town. I didn't find any sign of the woman who'd gone missing. I have more questions than answers."

"Zak said the same thing when he'd visited the Den," Jamie said. "He never did get Mac to trust him enough to tell him what, though."

"I'll find out," Logan swore. "I'll get to the bottom of it and find Samantha."

"I got a little more on her as well," Jamie said. "Cody Johnson was there when I spoke to Zak about Mac. He decided to take a little flight and flew over the troop."

"He didn't get caught?" Logan asked, immediately realizing what a stupid question that was. While he'd not met Cody, every Coalition agent knew who he was. There was even talk about making Cody the next director of the Coalition. The man was extremely talented. Even though many thought of the birds of prey species as being lesser than the larger predators, Logan knew better.

Jamie snorted. "They didn't have a clue he was there."

"Good."

"He did overhear some interesting conversations, though," Jamie said.

"Oh?"

"I wasn't actually certain that Frank hadn't done something with Samantha himself. It was just so tidy. His story."

"I had the same thought," Logan admitted.

"Well it seems Frank is really looking for Samantha and while she remains missing he's making her brother pay...

with blood."

"Shit," Logan spat.

"Yeah. We even considered saving him, but we sent out a few more spies and they called in that Samantha's brother actually sold her to Frank for a higher position in the troop."

"The fucker."

"Exactly," Jamie said. "They're only hurting him for now, so we're just watching, but if they try to kill him, the rescuer will swoop in."

"Anything else you can tell me?"

"This isn't the first time that Samantha has taken off on Frank. If she's running and has the help of Mac Gordon, I don't know if we'll find her."

"We may not want to, you mean."

"Yes," Jamie agreed.

"I'll think about it," Logan said. "I'm not done with Brookside, though. I want to know what is going on."

"Just be careful. We really don't know what is going on."

"I will be," Logan assured his friend.

"I'm sorry about this." Jamie lowered his voice. "I wish I hadn't called you. I don't want you getting into trouble."

Logan couldn't agree with that statement. Not that he planned to get in the middle of trouble, but he wasn't sorry about Jamie calling him. The flash of a beautiful, black-haired, green-eyed woman was in his thoughts. No, he didn't regret getting the call.

"Logan?"

Shit! He'd gotten lost in his thoughts again about Annabelle. "Sorry, was thinking about something."

"Something or someone?" Jamie asked.

"What?" There was no way that Jamie knew about Annabelle. Was Jamie having Logan followed as well?

"Relax," Jamie said with a chuckle. "I remember the beginning when I first met Brandy."

"Oh," he mumbled. Logan had a feeling he was blushing, so he was really glad he was all alone in his kitchen.

"I take it you met her in Brookside?"

"Yes," Logan admitted.

"Well at least she knows about shifters or is one."

"She is. Not sure what type, but a feline."

"I'm happy for you." Jamie sounded it, too.

"Getting ahead of yourself," Logan said. "I don't know anything about her or what she's into."

Jamie sighed. "Can I give you some advice?"

"Uh, I guess so."

"Trust your instincts."

Logan laughed. "That's it?"

"It's not as easy as it seems," Jamie assured him. "Your training, job, friends, something might try to get in the way. You're a powerful shifter, trust in what your animal tells you."

"Okay." Logan still didn't understand. "I'll do my best."

"If you need anything just give me a call."

"Thanks," Logan said. "Keep me informed on what the troop is up to."

"You got it."

Once Jamie hung up, Logan tossed his cell on the table. He stared back at his monitor.

Annabelle Sanchez.

He double-clicked the attachment to open it.

Logan lifted his mug and took a sip of cold coffee. "Ick." He spat the chilled brew into the cup and rose. *Disgusting.*

Crossing the room to start another pot and clean his mug, Logan thought about his next move. He had to return to Brookside. That much was obvious, but should he go under the guise of still searching for Samantha or should he warn Mac and Annabelle that the troop was looking for her?

Maybe he'd play it by ear? Logan set his mug in the sink and turned on the hot faucet before pulling the coffee pot closer. The familiar routine of pouring water, adding beans and turning on the machine calmed him. He shut off the water tap to stare out of the window above the sink. The view wasn't fantastic. He was on the third floor, overlooking a park.

Everything might be changing, but Logan was used to having to roll with the twists and turns of life.

The aroma of fresh, expensive coffee brewing filled the small room. He glanced around the apartment's small but tidy kitchen. It wasn't much, but he kept it spotless, filled with more food than he'd be able to eat and expensive décor. A far cry from the hole he'd once had to suffer. The roaches that had crawled on every inch of the avocado-green kitchen of the trailer were just one portion of the filth he'd lived in. Logan knew he'd paid too much for the place he currently resided in, but it was in one of the best buildings in the town. He didn't care about the money. He was never going to have to beg, borrow and steal to survive ever again.

He walked to his computer and sat. The file had opened. Was he really going to read all about Annabelle? Invade her privacy?

Yes, he was.

Logan began to scroll through the information.

A foster child.

Annabelle had grown up in group homes and temporary houses from age three to fourteen. At fourteen, she'd run away from the residence she'd been sent to and no one had heard from her again until she was eighteen and a legal adult.

She'd been questioned about her whereabouts for four years, but she'd refused to answer, instead only asking for her birth certificate and social security card. The government hadn't had a reason not to comply with her request.

At eighteen, she'd begun her life.

Logan had a feeling he knew where she'd spent those lost four years. Mac Gordon had to have had a hand in Annabelle's disappearance. Which didn't seem strange when he'd met the bear shifter while looking for another young woman.

The links were starting to come together and Logan didn't know what to think about it. Was Mac running some kind of halfway house for lost shifter girls?

Logan opened the Coalition database and typed in Annabelle's parents' names. She had to have ended up in the foster care system for a reason.

He frowned when the results came up empty. Logan typed the names again but received the same response.

That couldn't be possible. He switched to the FBI and tried again.

Nothing.

He had to log in to the CIA. As he waited for the website, he stood then crossed to the coffee pot. Logan pulled down a clean mug from the cabinet and poured some of the brew before taking the cup back to the table. His page had loaded, so he returned to work.

Annabelle's parents had to have left some sort of footprint in the past. A driver's license, a tax return—something.

Entering information into the CIA form was always time-consuming. He'd possibly cut down on the headache by using his less than legal means. Just a quick call and he'd have everything he could ever want on Annabelle and everyone related to her. He might even get the answers to what she was doing now.

No. Logan wouldn't go that route. Not only would it put him in debt once again, but it would also put Annabelle within reach of a scarier existence. No. Logan would dig the information out the old-fashioned way. By working the case.

After barely sleeping the previous night and a long, boring day of working the bar, Annabelle finally had the results of what Carter had been able to find about Logan. It had taken much longer than she'd expected. Carter had been thrilled, but the difficulty of hacking into the Coalition's system had gotten Annabelle annoyed. She wanted to know what Logan was up to and find out how to get him to leave them alone.

Finally, Annabelle had the pages in front of her that might

give her the Intel she needed to use against Logan.

Annabelle locked her bedroom door before sauntering to her favorite chair. She dropped down in the recliner and tucked her legs under her to open up the manila envelope Carter had passed her.

The first page was a full-sized photo taken the day Logan had graduated from the Phoenix police department. He'd been much younger, with innocence in his gaze that she hadn't seen in person. The years that had passed had been kind to Logan. He'd filled out in all the best ways. His face was fuller, with deep lines around his eyes and mouth. She wasn't sure they came from smiling, though. Logan seemed to be more the brooding and scowling type. Still, he looked mouthwateringly good in that uniform.

Instead of putting the picture in the envelope, Annabelle set it on the small table next to her. She'd decide what to do about it later. The next page had information about Logan's childhood. He'd grown up in a small town in Texas, close to the Mexico border.

Logan had been a decent student, making grades that were enough to get him through school, but not much better. His father had spent time in and out of jail. Hell, even his mom had a record. Annabelle closed her eyes. She had a feeling that Logan's early years might have been as bad as her own. She'd somehow not considered that he was more than just a Coalition agent.

He was also a man who had a past.

From the numerous trips he'd made to the hospital between the ages of five and ten, Annabelle suspected that Logan might know exactly how it felt to be alone and scared.

Opening her eyes again, she scanned Logan's teenage years, not wanting to see any more of his pain until he'd turned eighteen.

The last few months of high school, he'd buckled down and brought up his grades enough to be accepted into the police academy. He hadn't stuck around Texas, though.

Instead it appeared that he'd jumped on the first bus out of town and had never looked back.

He'd excelled at the police academy.

Logan had been at the top of the class during the entire training. By the time graduation had come, Logan already had an offer to work in Phoenix, but he hadn't accepted. Instead, he'd gone to California to join the Los Angeles Sheriff Department.

Then, he'd accepted one of the first posts for the Shifter Coalition.

Since he'd become an agent, Logan had gone after shifters who'd broken the law. From the case summaries she read, it seemed as though Logan took his job very seriously and he didn't quit. In one investigation, he'd tracked the criminal shifter for over six months.

That did not bode well for them if Logan found out about them. From all appearances, he was strictly by the book. There was no way he'd look the other way when it came to people disappearing. Even if it was for the best.

Some of the shifters they'd helped had spotty backgrounds. Mac always made sure that they helped the innocent, but that meant there were times when it went against the law.

Annabelle shook her head. She hadn't wanted to admit she'd been hoping to find something that told her she should trust Logan. Her attraction to him wouldn't keep her from being able to protect her family.

Logan was nothing but trouble. The evidence was in her hands. Annabelle shoved the printed sheets of paper into the envelope before standing. She shoved the package into the desk drawer and wandered to gaze out of her bedroom window. From there, she had the perfect view of the back of the property.

The woods behind the bar called to her and she saw her favorite tree from where she stood. Not all felines climbed, but her animal, a margay, was one of the most skillful of any species. The instincts that came along with her shifter abilities were strong in both human and cat form, but when she transformed, she never managed to stay out of the trees.

Annabelle released the catch on the window, unlocking it and pushing the pane up. Mac hated when she crawled out of her room this way, but Annabelle rather enjoyed it. She undressed quickly, scattering clothes along the floor before jumping out through the small opening.

Trent whirled around and cursed when she surprised him by landing only a few feet away from where he leaned against the back door. "Damn it, Annabelle!"

She merely grinned in response. Sure, she hadn't known he was out there, but she'd have fun sneaking up on the ex-cop. "Sorry," she lied.

"No you're not." He waved his hand at her. "And I thought Mac told you to stop doing that."

Annabelle shrugged. "It's faster this way."

"Tree calling you?" he asked, instead of continuing to lecture.

"Yeah," she replied. "It's a nice night."

"It is," he said. "But you still need to be careful. Mac is still worried about the fox troop showing up."

"I know." She pointed to her favorite spot. "I'm just going right there."

"Okay." Trent peered around the empty backyard. "Go ahead and shift and I'll keep an eye out for you."

"You don't have to. I might be out there a while." Her branch was the best place to think. Sometimes she even fell asleep.

"I don't mind," he said. "Not really tired, but I'm off duty until tomorrow afternoon."

Trent wouldn't bother her, she knew, and he often spent hours outside on his own. Annabelle thought it had something to do with his hyena nature but hadn't ever asked. Trent had joined the group after she'd already arrived, but she'd been a teen and hadn't been told his whole story.

That was the way things went with their little family. All of them had a reason for living out in the middle of nowhere in a town where they were surrounded by shifters or those who already knew and accepted them.

She had a feeling that Trent's past was full of pain and suffering. He went looking for trouble, which drove Mac crazy, but Trent never put anyone other than himself in danger. Mac let Trent have as much free rein as anyone, but Mac also kept a close eye on him. It was as if Mac was waiting for the day that Trent walked away from them. Annabelle hoped she was wrong, but in her gut she knew that Trent was just biding his time until he found whatever he was searching for.

The selfish part of her wanted to keep Trent with them, though. He was so gentle and kind to her.

"Go." He waved his hand. "It'll be fine."

Since he was giving her the chance to shift and still remain safe, avoiding a lecture from Mac, Annabelle was going to take him up on his offer. "Okay, but if you want to go inside at any time, it's fine."

Tent shook his head.

He was apparently done talking.

Annabelle closed her eyes so she'd be able to concentrate on the animal within. There was always a part of her that remained aware of her feline. Feeling the thread that ran between her human and feline sides, she mentally tugged at the connection. Warmth filled her as she began to transform.

There was no pain. Not since she'd learned to call her cat instead of losing control over her other form.

The snap of bones were loud and she arched as her body changed. She ignored all the noise around her until she was on all four paws and fur covered her. The chill of the night diminished with the thick coat covering her body.

Margays were unique to the shifter world. Even natural margays were uncommon. Annabelle didn't remember her mom or dad, any family really, so she'd researched their natural instincts and habitats to learn about herself.

The first time she'd read about how her species preferred

to stay in trees and, unlike many other felines, remained nocturnal, she finally felt the missing pieces in her soul connecting.

Annabelle had devoured every bit of information she'd found about the species. Mac had helped when he'd been able to, but not a lot was known about them. Studies were still going on and as much as Annabelle would love to travel to southern Mexico to see the natural cats, she didn't want to leave her family.

It had been a tough choice.

Everything inside her screamed to go and learn about her animal half. She should be solitary, that was ingrained in her species, but Annabelle craved the bonds of family. Even if that meant having to let go of finding out where she might have come from.

Annabelle stretched her forelegs out in front of her before arching her back. It felt so good. She loved shifting.

Trent smiled down at her when she looked up. Annabelle padded to him to wrap around one of his legs then the other. She marked him with her scent as a brother, a sibling of sorts, to show him love.

"Good kitty." He leaned down to pat her on the head.

She swiped a paw at him, but he moved deftly out of the way.

"Now go have fun."

Annabelle kneaded his leg with her sharp claws.

Using his other foot, he pushed her off. The shoelace of his boot was undone and she swatted at it. When he jerked his leg away, she pounced and followed that little piece of string.

She'd get it. She could. All she had to do was keep her eye on...

"Annabelle!"

She yowled in surprise. She hadn't meant to get distracted.

"I know," he said.

With one last head-butt to his knee, Annabelle took off at a sprint across the yard. At night, the northern California temperature dropped, but she wasn't feeling the cold. Instead, as she ran, her muscles heated and the feeling of freedom soared inside her. She didn't head directly to her tree. Instead, she sped past it, farther into the woods.

She knew better than to wander too far. In a town full of shifters, she wasn't one who'd fight some of the bigger predators. While conflict was unusual, Annabelle had to be careful. She wasn't as powerful as some of the others and she knew it. While they remained aware and still had human sensibilities while shifted, their animal instincts were stronger in that state. There'd been times when a shifter had let their animal nature take over, causing problems.

As she zigzagged between the trees, Annabelle had to keep her senses open and aware of her surroundings. It helped that she lived with several shifters who were considered large predators, Mac in particular. A grizzly bear shifter, Mac had gone toe-to-toe with numerous other shifters and had always come out on top. Not without injuries, but he was a formable opponent. His scent surrounded her, marking her as off limits.

Annabelle circled around, heading closer to the bar. Slowing down, she enjoyed the quietness of the forest around her. The full canopies of the trees hid the moon, allowing only small slivers to shine through. The damp ground cushioned her paws as she stepped carefully around twigs and fallen branches. It was such a beautiful night.

Maybe she would sleep in her tree, after all.

She'd made a sort of nest on one of the wide branches, against the trunk. After a bad day, or when the loneliness threatened to swamp her, she took refuge up high, where few could reach her in either human or shifter form.

The sound of a shotgun booming had Annabelle dropping low.

There weren't supposed to be any hunters in the area. The forest was a protected national park, the reason why it was safe for them to shift there.

When shifters had announced their presence and come out to the world, the hunting laws had become strict to ensure that shifters were not hunted down. Several humans had fought against the new regulations, but the government had been adamant that all shifters be protected, even in their animal form. In Annabelle's opinion, the new guidelines had been the best thing about the shifter announcement. Still, people could be stupid and that included hunting where they shouldn't.

She needed to get out of the way.

There was no doubt Trent and some of the others would have also heard the gunfire. Since Trent knew she was out, he'd come after her, and she didn't want anyone hurt on her behalf.

Staying as low to the ground as possible, she started to crawl toward the big round tree trunk just in front of her.

Another shot, and this time it seemed to be closer.

Ignoring the trembling she couldn't control, Annabelle scrambled forward faster. While she was quick as a feline, she couldn't take the chance of popping out of cover until she reached the tree and could go up. Not knowing who was out in the woods with her, Annabelle had to use her brain and not let instinct take over.

Relief flooded her when she felt rough bark against her paw. She just needed to go up. She jerked her head at the rustling coming up behind her. Three scents, and they were human. She wanted to snarl and growl, but that would give away her position.

"I'm telling you," a small, skinny, redheaded young man said. "I saw it. It looked like a cheetah or something. Just smaller."

Annabelle almost scoffed. She didn't look anything like a cheetah. Dumb humans.

The big, round, bald human slapped the redhead on the back. "You probably saw a fox or something, son."

Now she was really offended. She actually wanted to run at them so they got a good look at her. However, that would be a very bad idea. Not with those big guns in their hands.

"Do you think we scared it away?" the youngest, a black-haired teenager asked.

"I told you not to shoot until you had it in the crosshairs of your scope," Baldy said.

"Sorry, Dad," the redheaded man replied. "I got excited."

Enough was enough. Annabelle was irritated and pissed off. If she didn't do something, her family would come searching for her and they might come in shifted form.

She couldn't climb from her spot—the angle would give her away to the humans. If she moved, they might see her. Stuck, she went through her options. She could make a break for it. It seemed like at least two of the humans weren't marksmen, but the bald man might be. If she began the transformation, she'd be vulnerable if they didn't know what she was doing. Crap. She didn't know what to do.

"Let me see the flashlight," Baldy demanded.

A steak of light landed right on her.

"Holy shit!" the redhead shouted. "I told you." He lifted his rifle and Annabelle had to act.

Using her back legs, she launched herself at the tree and started to climb. Her claws scored the rough bark as she scrambled up, using the branches and leaves as cover.

Several birdshot shotgun rounds thudded in her wake.

She yelped when a pellet or ricochet hit her back leg. *No, no, no.* She couldn't get killed by a bunch of moronic humans.

Annabelle's foot slipped on a branch and she cried out, barely catching herself.

"There! Up there!" someone called.

The humans fired several more times.

Finding a small opening, Annabelle dove for it. She wedged herself in, hoping it would hide her. She was high enough that as long as the humans didn't have a direct shot, she should be okay.

The loud, long growl that shook the entire area around her was both a relief and filled her with terror. Mac was coming and he'd be coming in as a bear.

Logan heard the first shot as he closed the door of his truck behind him. Instinct took over and he raced toward the back of the bar, gun in hand, before he realized what he was doing.

He rounded the corner and spotted another man in the yard, running in the direction of the woods. The bar's rear door flew open and Logan aimed at the figure stepping out.

"Annabelle!" the guy in the yard yelled. "She's out there!"

Cold dread filled Logan. He now recognized that it was Mac exiting the building. "Where?"

The stranger and Mac both looked at him in surprise. They hadn't even known he was there.

Another gunshot.

"Trent," Mac said calmly. "Is she in her tree?"

"No," Trent cried. "She went for a run first."

Mac glanced at Logan. "We have to find her."

"Any idea who's out there?" Logan asked. He didn't holster his weapon, instead lowering it by his side.

"Probably hunters," Mac said. "The forest is protected, but that doesn't keep everyone out."

"Fuck," Logan spat.

"Trent," Mac said. "Go ahead and try to find her. Stay in human form so you don't get shot."

Trent didn't hesitate. He took off at full speed.

"Going to call this in, agent?" Mac asked.

"You have a sheriff around here?"

"Yes."

"Call him," Logan said. "I'm going to find out what's going on."

"Carter!" Mac yelled. "Call this in. We'll be in the woods."

Logan started forward but stopped and frowned when Mac yanked his shirt over his head.

"Is that wise?" Logan asked. "If it's hunters?"

"I said it's *probably* hunters," Mac corrected. "If it's not…"

While Mac let his sentence trail off, he finished undressing.

From farther away, they heard yet another shot, then a faint yelp. Mac roared and it actually shook the ground under Logan's feet. But, Jesus, the man's power radiated from him.

"Go!" Mac ordered, crouching.

Logan didn't need to be told twice. At a pace slower than Trent had taken off, he jogged toward the tall tree line. *Is this what Annabelle has to worry about? She can't even go for a run without having to watch for bullets?*

What would they have done if he hadn't been there?

It appeared they had faced this situation all ready. Hopefully, that would keep Annabelle safe.

Annabelle. He hadn't been able to keep her out of his thoughts, as he'd spent his day investigating the town and its residents. He'd driven through the town in circles before parking and getting out. He'd been inside every store and spoken to every person he passed, showing Samantha's picture around.

There was no way that many people had lied to him. Samantha was not there. That he was sure of.

Even with his badge, the citizens of Brookside had been wary of him, but they'd answered every question. Logan was beginning to think that Samantha had never been there at all. He'd headed to the bar to question the two men who'd supposedly picked up the young fox shifter. Instead, he now found himself stepping into the dark forest, hoping to find Annabelle safe.

The moonlight disappeared as soon as he entered. The temperature also dropped by several degrees. There was no movement, no sound, and that worried him. The natural creatures that called the woods their home would have been scared by the shots, but he couldn't hear the humans either.

There were a couple of scents he'd be able to follow.

Logan didn't know what type of shifter Trent was, but his trace had to be the more recent aroma. Instead of following him, Logan closed his eyes and thought about Annabelle.

Her unique feline-tinted scent. Yes, picturing her in his

mind helped him remember how she smelled. Straight ahead. Maybe a half hour to an hour ago.

Logan marched forward with determined strides.

He prayed he didn't hear any more gunfire. If he got there in time, he'd make sure that the hunters were dealt with accordingly. The new laws were in effect for a reason. But, sometimes, they didn't protect everyone. Logan sped up. He wouldn't let anything happen to Annabelle while he was out here. No. It was his job to protect shifters and he couldn't fail.

Logan began to jog.

Behind him came a crash of branches and he had a feeling that Mac had completed his shift and was now coming. Logan couldn't think about that, though. He knew Mac and apparently Trent cared about Annabelle, but he had to be there to help her.

It didn't make sense. This was more than him wanting to help another shifter. Every instinct inside him screamed that he shift and protect her. He wanted to prove that he'd keep her safe. Which was fucking insane. Logan didn't even know her, but it was his lion driving him forward, more than his human side.

"*No!*"

Logan heard the shout and turned toward the sound, slightly left of his current location, and ran. It appeared Annabelle had run pretty much in a straight line.

A young red-haired man flew through the air as Logan stepped around a tree.

"Stop or I'll shoot!" A big bald guy was pointing his rifle at Trent, who held a teenager off the ground by his neck.

"Do it," Trent growled. "I'll rip his fucking head off."

"Nobody move," Logan said, stepping forward. He picked up the badge from his back pocket. "US Shifter Coalition." With his weapon trained on the bald man, he held his identification up with the other hand. "Drop your weapon."

The bald man paled but didn't comply. "I'm not dropping

anything until he lets my son go."

Trent bared his fangs at the teenager.

"Drop it now," Logan demanded. "And he'll let go of your boy."

The human appeared to know he wasn't going to get his way and dropped the rifle.

"Kick it toward me," Logan ordered.

The bald man did so and Logan spotted the other two guns close by.

"Now drop to your knees and link your fingers behind your head," Logan told him.

"Tell that animal to let go of my son," Baldy shouted. "We weren't doing anything wrong. He had no right to attack. I want him arrested."

"What were you shooting at?" Logan asked. He closed the distance between him and the human.

"We were hunting," Baldy replied with a lift of his chin.

"This area is protected. It's part of the national forest. There is no hunting here," Logan stated.

"There's no hunting anywhere!" Baldy exclaimed. "Not since those animals got their way."

What an idiot. Logan almost pointed out that he was one of those animals, but didn't see the point.

"Get down on your knees," Logan repeated.

Mac growled as he appeared at Logan's side, making the bald man lower himself to the ground and cover his head.

"Jesus!" Baldy yelled. "There are more of them!"

Logan eyed him, but he seemed calm enough, so he turned toward Trent. "Release the boy."

With yellow eyes shining, Trent shook the teenager instead. "Where were you aiming?"

"There." The teenager's fingers shook as he pointed up at the tree.

Logan narrowed his eyes but couldn't see through the thick branches and leaves.

Trent growled but let the kid go. The teenager scrambled quickly away from Trent to his father's side.

"Take the same position," Logan said to the boy. After they were side by side, he glanced at the redhead, who seemed to still be out. His chest moved up and down. The young man lived.

"Annabelle!" Trent called softly. "You up there?"

Logan couldn't see anything but the scent... "I smell blood."

This time the rumbling came from Mac.

There was a sharp, poignant scent and Mac realized the teenager had pissed his pants. Smart boy—he should be scared.

Mac took a few unsteady steps toward the humans, but Logan held up his hand. They didn't need any more conflict.

"Annabelle!" Trent said louder.

Above their heads, there was movement before a small brown head with black rosettes and streaks peeked down at him. Her eyes were wide with terror, but she was the most beautiful creature he'd ever seen.

Chapter Four

Annabelle stared at the men below her. Three humans and three shifters. Mac was in his bear form while Trent stood under the branch she hid in. It was Logan, though, who she couldn't take her gaze from. He looked good in a pair of tan pants and a blue button-down shirt. Her sharp eyesight helped her see his handsome face as he looked back at her. There was concern in his gaze, as though Logan worried for her.

What's he doing here? Has he come with the humans? No, that didn't make sense. He had to have been with Mac or Trent. Maybe he'd been inside the bar?

All the questions were giving her a headache and that was on top of the throbbing pain in her leg. Annabelle placed her chin over the edge of the trunk.

"Are you okay?"

It was Logan who asked the question, but she scented the fear from Trent and Mac as well. She trilled softly in response. She would be fine as long as they didn't expect her to move anytime soon. She ached and just wanted to sleep now that the danger was over.

"What...why...are you talking to the cat?" the teenager asked. "Does it understand you?"

"She," Logan said.

Annabelle wanted to smile when Logan corrected the boy. It was a small thing, but she hated being called an *it*.

"She," the teen repeated.

"The reason hunting is illegal here is because the shifters run in this forest. You almost killed a person," Logan explained. It sounded as though this wasn't the first time he'd had to explain.

The boy began to shake, but his father snorted. "Filthy animals. That's all they are."

Annabelle wanted to leap down and bite the stupid human dad.

The teenager turned to his father. "But you said when they turned into animals they weren't human anymore. They spoke to that cat and she responded."

"It's a trick," Baldy replied. "You can't trust these men. They might look like us, but they're not."

Damn. Annabelle's stomach rolled. This wasn't just a couple of men out for some fun. This man had known there was a chance that he'd be hunting a shifter. They'd really tried to kill her.

"We need the sheriff here now." Logan looked at Mac as he spoke.

Mac nodded then peered up at Annabelle. She blinked her eyes and nodded. He could go. She was safe in her tree. He left with one last look at Trent. Words weren't needed. Not even when it was a bear staring at them. The humanity in Mac's gaze was noticeable and he was putting Trent in charge of her.

She wiggled around a little to get a better view of what was happening behind her. Logan gathered those big rifles that had been pointed at her.

"Will you come down?" Trent asked her.

She shook her head. That didn't sound like a good idea at all.

Trent sighed. "You know I can't climb up there to get you."

Annabelle did. Trent didn't like heights and when he shifted to his hyena he couldn't climb at all. There was nothing to worry about, though. She'd come down when she was ready.

"Can you help me move this guy?" Logan called to Trent.

Trent grinned up at her before turning to the agent. Annabelle watched them work together. Trent picked up the young red-haired man while Logan covered the other two. The humans remained quiet, but Annabelle easily saw that the teenager was still upset. Good. Maybe this would be a lesson for him.

The bald man was silent, but she could still pick up on his hatred. Trent lowered the young man between his father and brother and the shifters backed off. It was smart of Logan not to turn his back on him. The man was angry and it would be easy for him to act out. Especially with the sheriff coming.

"Will you let the sheriff handle this?" Trent whispered.

Annabelle heard, but she doubted that the humans would.

"I'm going to have him take them in for the night. This is a federally protected land so it does fall under my jurisdiction. The federal charges will be stiffer, so I'll for sure charge the dad with those."

"Good," Trent said. He glanced at her. "They might've killed Annabelle."

She hated the fear in Trent's voice. It wasn't fair. All she'd wanted to do was spend some time in her tree. The run earlier hadn't been needed, but she enjoyed the forest.

"I'll make sure they never do anything like this again," Logan said. "How often do you have to deal with illegal hunting?"

Trent chuckled before sitting on a log across from the humans. "Not a lot. Once word got around about shifters, we had several hate groups stalking all the wooded areas in the state, but it's died down. At least I think it has. Normally the hunters don't come out this far."

"That's good."

"Yeah, we keep guards around the property and if we shift as a group we always have sentries ready, but with a town full of shifters, it can be dangerous. It's not like we can have set times when someone wants to transform. Annabelle's species is nocturnal, so she prefers to change at night."

"Is she an ocelot?" Logan asked.

Annabelle yowled in response.

Both shifters laughed.

"Guess not," Logan said.

"She's a margay," Trent said. He stared up at her with a smirk.

Annabelle didn't know what that look was about, but she felt it had something to do with Logan.

"Margay?" Logan repeated. "I haven't heard of that species before. Which I guess isn't really surprising. There are hundreds of different feline types."

That's an understatement, Annabelle wanted to say. It hadn't been easy to find out where she'd come from. With no family or anyone who knew about her, Annabelle had always felt as if she missed something important about herself.

"Lion, right?" Trent asked. "I thought at first you might be a panther, but now I'm pretty sure your scent is lion."

"Yes," Logan confirmed.

Annabelle had known from the start was type of shifter Logan was. She closed her eyes again as the two men quietly discussed the different species that Logan worked with. She liked Logan's deep, soft voice. His caring tone washed over her, helping to remove the last bits of fear.

She wondered again what he was doing there. After looking through his file earlier, Annabelle had wanted to get him out of her head. He was by the book. Dedicated to his mission. There was no way that he'd fit in with their ragtag group. Logan didn't belong in the middle of nowhere with them as they spent their days in the shadows of an underground world. He had to enjoy the spotlight. Annabelle couldn't see why a shifter would join the Coalition if they weren't interested in recognition.

The Shifter Coalition might have been founded with the purpose of helping the shifter communities in the push to get equal rights and stop discrimination, but Annabelle hadn't seen a whole lot of that. Instead, going by the news she'd seen on television and articles online, it appeared to her that the Coalition policed the shifters more than helped. It was a betrayal, to her.

If Samantha had had the option of fighting against her troop leader, then her life would have been so different. She might not have lost her first baby.

But the Coalition didn't help the low pack members against the evil leaders. Instead the organization was all about the law. She needed to keep reminding herself of that fact. Logan wasn't there for any other reason than to work his investigation. Annabelle and her family were nothing more than suspects to him.

"Coming in!" Mac called out and Annabelle lifted her head while Trent stood.

Mac, Carter and Sheriff Magnus stepped into view. Logan strode toward the sheriff.

"Agent Coldwell." Logan held out his hand to the sheriff. "Thanks for coming."

Sheriff Magnus was a big guy, at least six foot three and over two hundred and fifty pounds. He was a tiger shifter and intimated the hell out of Annabelle. Although he had always been kind to her, Annabelle couldn't get past the dominance that radiated from him.

"Glad I was able to be of service," Magnus said gruffly. "What have we got?"

"Seems our friend here," Logan waved at the bald dad, "decided it didn't matter that hunting is illegal here or that they'd be firing at a shifter."

"They knew?" Magnus asked. He glared at the bald man. "You sure?"

"Oh yeah," Logan answered. "I have no doubt."

"How do you want me to handle it?" Magnus crouched next to the guy who was still passed out.

"If you'll take them to your station, I'll come down and make recommendations," Logan said. "I'll be filing federal charges on the dad here."

"You can't do that!" Baldy yelled. He turned his gaze to Magnus. "You're the sheriff and I want to make a compliant." Baldy pointed at Trent. "He attacked us."

"Is that true?" Magnus asked Trent.

"Since they'd been shooting at Annabelle and were seconds away from firing again? Yes, I stopped them," Trent said.

Magnus shook his head before addressing the human. "You got lucky. He might have killed you."

"Fuck," Baldy spat. "You're one of them."

Magnus grinned and yanked Baldy up. "Yeah, and now you're coming with me."

"What about my son?"

Trent leaned down and easily hefted the red-haired man onto his shoulder. Annabelle was really starting to worry about how long he'd been out. *Wait!* No, she didn't care. He had tried to kill her.

Damn, I can't actually be that cold.

"Cuffs?" Logan asked.

Magnus tossed him a package with zip-tie restraints. Logan caught them then helped the teenager to his feet. Logan was a lot gentler with the kid than Magnus was with the dad.

"Where's Annabelle?" Magnus asked.

She ducked her head out of the way.

"Up the tree," Trent said. "She hasn't come down yet."

"We'll need to talk to her," Magnus stated.

"I'll take care of it," Logan said. "Let's get these guys out of here first. She might feel more comfortable then."

Annabelle wasn't hiding because of the humans. She just didn't want to deal with everything. It wasn't her fault the idiots had been shooting at her. Plus, she was going to have to talk to Magnus and Logan.

If she didn't find a way to overcome her attraction to the lion shifter, Annabelle would make a fool of herself. He was an agent who would be more than happy to put Calvin or Duffy in jail. Hell, he'd probably want to take her and Mac in as well if he found out they'd lied to him.

"I'll stay and keep her company," Carter offered.

Annabelle made a sound of protest. She didn't need anyone to stay with her.

"He'll stay," Mac called up to her. "When you're ready, come back. We need to look you over."

Oh yeah, she was bleeding from her leg. She waved her front paw at him.

"I think she's flipping you off," Magnus joked.

"Don't make me come up there," Mac threatened.

She knew he wouldn't, though. As big as he was, Mac couldn't reach her. But he might have Carter climb. In human form, the smaller shifter was a pretty good climber, although he didn't enjoy it like she did.

"We're just going to leave her here?" Logan asked.

"She'll be fine," Mac assured him.

Annabelle had the urge to look over the branch to see his face but decided that would only give Mac more ammunition to force her down.

It took several minutes, but finally everyone else was trekking through the forest, leaving her alone with Carter.

"I really wish you'd come down so I can look at you," Carter said. "We don't have to go back yet."

She huffed but started to climb out of the hole she'd found. Annabelle was going to have to mark this tree as her own. It had saved her life, so she should return. Her back leg shot pain angrily up to her spine and she whimpered.

"Shit! Annabelle?"

Annabelle clamped her teeth together so she wouldn't worry Carter any further. It was a lot harder to balance on three legs than all four. Every time she tried to put her full weight on her leg, it hurt, so she limped from branch to branch until she was on the lowest.

Carter stood at the bottom of the tree, looking up at her. "I'll catch you."

He was small but held shifter strength. Annabelle debated. Just climbing from her spot had been tiring and she didn't want to attempt going down the trunk with only three good paws.

She nodded.

"On three," he said. "One…two…three."

Annabelle pushed off and leaped into his open arms. He closed his strong limbs around her, warming her up and comforting her all at the same time.

"It's okay," he murmured. "You're okay." Carter carried her to the same log that Trent had sat on. He dropped down before moving to cradle her between his legs. "Let's take a look."

His hands were gentle, but she still hissed when he tugged at her back leg.

"Sorry" he murmured. "It doesn't look like you were hit by a bullet. I think it's only a graze."

Which meant that she wouldn't be in pain for long. While shifters didn't heal instantly like they did in movies or books, they did have a better healing rate than humans. Something to do with the transforming back and forth helped to speed up nature. The DNA that allowed them to shift also took care of injuries.

"It might scar, but you'll look like a badass," Carter warned her.

Annabelle swiped at his face but kept her claws in. He was just teasing her, but if she didn't put up some sort of fight, he'd think something was wrong.

All she really wanted was to be cuddled.

As if he'd heard her thoughts, Carter lifted her until her head was under his chin. Annabelle purred as he began to knead the nape of her neck. His hands felt good, his scent familiar and just what she needed.

Family.

That was what Carter was to her. In his embrace, she didn't have to worry about what was going to happen next. Mac would probably lecture her, Trent would feel guilty and she was going to have to talk to Logan or Magnus.

Maybe she'd just stay as her feline for the rest of the night.

She pawed at Carter's head.

"I know you want to stay, but we really should head to

the bar," Carter said then rose.

Damn it. She wished she was a bird shifter, where she'd just fly away. Carter tightened his hold, although his hands remained gentle.

"Don't even think of taking off," he said. "Your leg has to get looked at."

Annabelle relaxed her muscles, letting Carter take her full weight. She was lucky to be small enough to carry. If it had been Trent, Carter or Mac who needed help, there was no way that any of them could carry one another like they did Annabelle.

As often as she'd wished she was bigger and more powerful, times like this really made her appreciate her species. She might be larger than a regular house cat, but Annabelle had picked up some of their habits since her family enjoyed playing with her in this form.

Carter dug his finger into the spot right above her shoulder blades and it felt like magic. Annabelle purred and just enjoyed the ride.

* * * *

Logan paced in front of the back door. The sheriff had taken the three suspects down to the station once the redhead had woken up. Now all he had to do was wait until Annabelle returned. He'd wanted to go back after her, but Mac had nixed that idea, saying she'd need a few minutes to get herself down.

He was more worried about what injuries she might have than anything else. Yes, he needed to speak to her and get her side of what had happened, but he'd smelled her blood, which was much more important.

"You need to be calm when she gets back," Mac said as he stepped outside to join Logan on the lawn.

"I'm calm," Logan responded.

Mac snorted. "I can feel your lion at the surface."

True, but Logan was in no danger of losing control. He

didn't lose control. "I can handle myself."

"I bet." Mac waved a hand toward a bench that Logan hadn't even noticed. "We'll have some time to talk while we wait."

Logan followed him and sat beside Mac.

"I didn't expect you back so soon," Mac said.

"Didn't you?" Logan challenged. "I know you're hiding something. I'm not certain if it has to do with my missing woman or not, but something is going on here."

Mac shook his head. "We're just a small town that takes care of ourselves."

"And don't trust the Coalition?"

"Not just the Coalition," Mac corrected. "Any law enforcement. A lot of the people here have a good reason why they don't, too."

"I'm not here to cause trouble," Logan assured him. And he wasn't. He was merely doing his job. If they kept freezing him out, though, he'd be forced to look into all the people Mac said didn't trust him. It would be their fault, because he wasn't going to just let this case go.

"Then why'd you come here and spend all day questioning the residents?" Mac asked.

"I'm trying to find a missing woman."

"Have you considered that she's missing for a reason? That maybe she had a reason to disappear?" Mac asked.

"Yes," Logan acknowledged. "From the intelligence that we're gathering, it is a distinct possibility. But so is something bad happening to her, and someone filed a missing person report to cover their ass."

Mac nodded. "Good point. Still, you're wasting your time here. That woman is not here."

"I believe you," Logan said. "But I still believe that someone here knows more than they're admitting." He was sure of it, in fact. Logan had been trained by the best. It was obvious that Mac and his little group were up to something. If he was honest with himself, his greatest concern was for Annabelle. What if she wasn't aware that her friends had secrets? She'd end up in real trouble.

"Perhaps," Mac conceded.

"So are you going to tell me what's going on around here?"

"I did," Mac said. "We live a quiet life. Except for a few instances like today."

"Fine," Logan said. "I'll figure it out." The vow was more to himself than a warning to Mac.

"Besides, if I told you," Mac said, "you wouldn't have a reason to keep turning up. Then what would you do?"

"Meaning?" Logan asked, although he had a suspicion he knew what Mac spoke about.

"Meaning you couldn't use your case as an excuse to see Annabelle."

Logan grinned. "Since you warned me away from her, I'd think that you'd want to tell me, so I wouldn't come back."

Mac chuckled as he stretched his long legs out in front of him while slouching down the bench. "I didn't warn you away. If you remember correctly, I told you I wouldn't have to."

That was true. Still, Logan couldn't decide if Mac wanted him chasing after Annabelle or not. The bear shifter was hard to read, which confused Logan, since he was pretty damn good at figuring people out.

"It's up to you whether you put in the time to get past Annabelle's defenses or not," Mac said. "Some have tried, but in the end they never stick around long enough."

"I'm not going anywhere," Logan said before he thought better of it. It was true that his attraction to Annabelle was strong, but he barely knew the woman. Hell, he'd just learned what species she was and knew nothing about what she needed.

"We'll see," Mac said, the disbelief heavy in his tone.

Yes, they would. He shouldn't be making promises that he wasn't sure he could keep. Eventually the case that had brought him to Brookside would be completed and he'd move on to his next investigation. Even if Annabelle felt a small amount of the attraction he did they'd still live an hour away from each other. Plus, there was always the chance of him getting called away.

Logan didn't respond out loud, though, because he'd picked up the faint sound of footsteps headed their way. From the forest. He and Mac both stood as Carter came out of the woods, holding Annabelle, still in feline form. The urge to shift was strong. In his lion form, she would naturally defer to him.

Instead, he clenched his jaw to remain in control. He hadn't been lying earlier when he'd told Mac he was calm. Logan was known to be cool under any circumstance. But there was a tendril of jealously that coursed through him when he noted how relaxed Annabelle was in Carter's arms.

Logan had scented the young man earlier and knew he wasn't a threat. The prey odor that came from Carter didn't even stir his lion. No—Carter was not a danger to him. Or Annabelle.

"She okay?" Mac called out over Annabelle's loud purring.

"She has a gash from what I suspect is the bullet grazing her, but she'll be fine," Carter stated.

The bullet grazed her? Logan vowed that he'd charge the damn hunter with every broken law he could think of. *How dare he try to kill her?*

"After she shifts back and takes a long shower, she'll be good as new," Carter said.

Logan wished he could reach over, pet Annabelle and feel her soft fur beneath his fingers.

It was Mac who took Annabelle, to cuddle her close. "Go ahead," he said to Logan. "She loves to be petted."

"Sure," Logan said. He was thankful his hand was steady as he carefully and slowly stroked the top of her head.

Annabelle responded with a long, deep moan. Mac chuckled as Logan pulled his hand away in surprise. He'd never heard a feline make that sound before.

"It's okay," Mac informed him. "That means she's really

happy."

Taking the bear shifter at his word, Logan returned his fingers to Annabelle's chin and scratched.

She allowed this for a few moments then slipped onto her back, still in Mac's arms, and batted at his hand. Logan stopped moving his fingers. She wrapped her paw around his wrist and pulled with strength until she had her teeth around the pad of one of his digits.

"Ouch," he complained when a sharp tooth dug in.

"Yeah." Mac tapped Annabelle's nose. "Sometimes I think she's more domesticated than she likes to admit."

With that comment, Annabelle swatted Mac's chin, drawing a laugh from Logan.

"I guess she really is okay," Logan said.

"Yes," Mac agreed. He handed her to Carter. "Take her to her room so she can shift back and clean up."

"Okay." Carter kissed the top of her head before turning to meander toward the rear entrance.

"Come," Mac said. "We'll have a beer while we wait on her."

Logan glanced at his watch. It had been a long day and he still had to make the drive home.

"We have a spare room you can use," Mac told him. "You'll have to turn around and be here in the morning to take care of the hunters."

"Later this morning," Mac corrected. It was after three already.

"Right," Mac said. "We're used to bar hours here."

"I think I'll take you up on your offer," Logan said. "It'll save me time."

"You have a bag in your truck?"

"Yes." Logan pulled his keys put of his pocket. "I'll get it and meet you in the bar."

Mac nodded and followed Carter through the back door. Logan decided to stay outside and strode off in the direction he'd come. It seemed like days had passed since he'd gotten out of his truck with the intention of questioning the bar patrons about Duffy and Calvin. Instead, mere hours had gone by and he was exhausted. It was really nice of Mac to put him up for the night.

Before he'd left his apartment, Logan had tried to find lodging in town. Brookside didn't have a hotel or even a bed and breakfast. Instead, the closest place he'd been able to find was forty minutes away. Which was a waste, since his drive was an hour long. He wouldn't throw away the money to save only twenty minutes' drive time.

However, he had packed up a bag, his laptop and files in case he found something once he got to town. Maybe they just didn't advertise. Logan hadn't been so lucky, though. It appeared that Brookside really did its best to keep strangers away.

Now, knowing they'd had trouble with hunters, Logan understood the need, although he still thought something more was going on.

Maybe he'd be able to get some information from the sheriff. Magnus had seemed like a good law enforcement ally. Logan hadn't wanted to involve the local police until he knew what was happening in the town, but he was past that now. Hopefully Magnus would be more forthcoming than Mac and the residents had been.

Logan reached his truck and pushed the Unlock button on the key fob before opening the back door. He'd had a safe installed in the rear floorboard to keep his weapon and other work-related items when he needed them. It was a trick he'd learned early in his career. He couldn't always take his work in with him but needed to keep it secure. Logan opened the safe and removed his laptop then closed the lid. He'd leave his files inside. He didn't need them at the moment.

He shoved the computer under his arm and grabbed his duffel off the seat. *That should be enough for now.*

After he slammed the door closed, he turned and almost ran into Trent.

"Fuck, man," Logan exclaimed. "Don't sneak up on me

like that."

Trent laughed. "I wasn't actually trying to. You seemed deep in thought."

Logan chuckled. "I think I'm more tired than I realized."

"Well, come on then," Trent said. "You can have a beer while we get a room ready for you."

He nodded and followed Trent toward the bar's front door. There weren't any other vehicles in the parking lot. "Is my truck safe here?"

"Yeah, no worries. We have security cameras and they're always monitored."

"Great," Logan said. He really did like his truck and didn't want it messed with. Since most of the residents had already seen him driving it around, they'd know who the vehicle belonged to.

"I'll take your bag," Trent said as they reached the entrance. "I think Mac's putting you in Calvin's old room."

"Old room?" Mac asked. "I thought Calvin lived here."

Trent chuckled as he pulled open the door. "He does, but he shares with Duffy now. They've been together for several years."

"Good, then." Maybe Calvin had left some things in his old residence that would give Logan a look at the other man. He was still Logan's main suspect in the disappearance of Samantha.

"He still keeps some stuff in the room, but you'll have plenty of space."

They stepped inside the bar. The lights were dim in the main room, but he spotted Mac sitting on a stool at the bar. He was alone, so Logan passed Trent his bag before walking to join the bear shifter.

"Poured you a beer," Mac said without turning around. The mirror behind the bar let him see Logan, although Mac had probably heard him approach just fine. His shoes creaked over the old wooden floor.

"I appreciate it," Logan said, sitting down beside him.

"I checked on Annabelle. She's in the shower and will join

us shortly. Then I suspect that you'll want to turn in."

Logan ran his hands roughly over his face. "Yeah."

Mac chuckled. "I don't envy you your job."

"It's usually not so exciting," Logan confessed. "A lot of arrests of shifters and humans breaking the law. Paperwork—fuck, the paperwork is a bitch. And appearing in court. We're actually pretty lucky up here. We haven't had the same hate groups form around here."

"I've read about some in Arizona, Texas and Colorado," Mac said. "It makes me glad I settled here."

"What made you decide on Brookside?" Logan questioned. He was honestly curious.

"Is it Agent Coldwell asking or Logan?"

"It's just me," Logan said. "A man having a beer."

Mac picked up his cold pilsner and seemed to steady it. Logan was about to change the subject, expecting Mac not to answer, when the bear shifter chuckled. "It was an accident."

"Accident?" he pressed.

"I'd just gotten out of the service and gained custody of Duffy. I'd been stationed in San Diego and planned on taking Duffy to Oregon or Washington State. I didn't want Duffy anywhere close to where his mom—my sister—died."

"I'm sorry," Logan said sincerely. "I read about her murder."

Mac dipped his head. "Thanks. So here I was, traveling through the state with Duffy, and my bike broke down. Ten miles from here."

"That sucks."

"Yeah," Mac said. "Luckily a passing jeep stopped to check on us. Alexander Santos, he owns the Italian restaurant in town. A master chef."

"I met him today," Logan confessed.

"He told me," Mac said. "He's still one of my best friends. Anyway, Alexander picked me and Duffy up and took us to his restaurant. He fed us and called a mechanic friend of his. It took three days to get my bike fixed. But when we were ready to get on the road, neither one of us wanted to leave."

"That's...surprising," Logan stated. "Not knowing anyone here."

"It was so different here," Mac said. "Every person I met was a shifter. We didn't have to hide who we were. It's freeing."

"I bet." Logan heard his own wistfulness.

"I had some money put aside from my time in the service and opened this place."

Logan peered around at the bar, which was quickly growing on him. It wasn't the kind of place where he'd usually stop to have a pint or relax. Now he regretted not giving establishments like this a chance. He was beginning to understand that it was the people who made the Den so remarkable.

A shuffling of feet came from behind him and he turned on his stool.

Annabelle stood in the doorway between the main bar floor and the kitchen. She was dressed simply in a pair of faded gray slacks and a white v-neck T-shirt. Her feet were bare and her toes were painted a pretty pink. With her long black hair cascading down in soft wet curls, she was a vision.

"Well." Mac rose. "I'll leave you two to talk, and call it a night."

Logan turned and nodded to him. "Thank you."

Mac walked quietly across the room. His big combat boots didn't even make the boards creak. Logan grinned. The bear shifter was still showing off, but Logan didn't mind.

He watched while Mac bent his head to speak softly to Annabelle before kissing her on the cheek and leaving them alone.

"Do you want a drink?" he offered.

"Isn't that my line?" she replied, taking the first steps forward.

"Yeah," Logan said and chuckled. "I guess it is."

She stopped beside him and he looked her over. She didn't appear to be injured — she just seemed tired, but it was the protectiveness on the surface he was having a hard time dealing with. His hands shook with the need to check every inch of her.

"How's your leg?"

Annabelle smiled at him. "It's fine. I put some ointment and a bandage over the gash and probably won't even know it was ever there by morning."

"You still could have been killed," Logan pointed out. "I need to talk to you about that."

"I don't really know anything about the men in the forest."

"I just need you to tell me what happened," Logan said.

"Okay." She climbed onto the stool that Mac had vacated. "I can do that."

Chapter Five

Annabelle tried to ignore the feeling of Logan so close by her side. She'd really enjoyed when he'd petted her earlier and wished she was in cat form so she could feel his fingers against her fur.

"Take your time," Logan said.

As she started her story, Logan pulled out a small notebook from his back pocket and took notes. It amused her that he carried around the pad. *He's the perfect little agent, isn't he?*

There wasn't a whole lot to tell and he only asked a few follow-up questions before he closed the cover and slipped his notebook into his pocket.

"That should take care of it for now," he said. "I suspect you're worn out."

She was, but Annabelle also didn't want to leave him yet. Now that she'd gotten the unpleasantness of the night over with, she wanted to talk to Logan. She just wasn't sure where to start. Well, there was one thing she still wondered.

"What were you doing here, anyway?" she asked.

Logan smiled before he picked up his beer and downed the rest. "Officially? I'm checking up on my case. I need to speak with Duffy and Calvin."

"Oh," she murmured. What had she expected? He wouldn't have come back just for her. She'd not given him any reason to think she was interested in him.

"You're supposed to ask me the unofficial reason," he commented.

Bossy bastard. That turned her on, though. "What's the unofficial reason?"

"I knew you'd be here," Logan said quietly. "Or at least

I hoped."

"Really?" The warmth that filled her was an unusual feeling, one that she'd feared for so long.

"I don't know why I just told you that," he admitted. He laughed, but it sounded different from the happy sound she'd heard before.

"I think it's nice," she assured him. It was great to not have to guess where his thoughts were. Since Annabelle remained unsure herself of the strong attraction between them, knowing that Logan was in the same boat helped. "I'm glad you came." It was her turn to be honest.

"Because I arrested the men who were shooting at you?" he asked.

Annabelle automatically shook her head. "No. I could have handled that. Or Trent or Mac would have, and after, they'd have called the sheriff. It was nice seeing you there, looking all fierce and protective."

"I feel protective toward you," he said quietly. "God only knows why. You can obviously take care of yourself."

"I can," she agreed. "But that doesn't mean it's not a comfort when someone worries or wants to help."

Logan turned on his stool a little more so they were facing each other. His knees bracketed hers and if she leaned forward just a few inches, they'd be touching. "I know you don't trust me."

She opened her mouth to argue but quickly closed it again. He was right and to dispute his statement would make her a liar.

"That's what I thought," he said. "But I can't stop thinking about you. I should be focused on my investigation, but instead all I wanted to do was come here and sit in front of this bar so I could watch you."

Annabelle had started dating when she'd been sixteen. The first time she'd had sex had been at nineteen. In all the times that she'd been interested in men, no one had ever reached that part of her heart that Logan currently tugged on. "I wish I could tell you what you want to know." The statement was true, and it was also all she could give him. It wasn't up to her to break the silent code about the underground group she was a part of.

"Maybe someday?" he questioned.

Annabelle finally closed the distance. She pressed her leg against his before placing her palm on his thigh. "We're good people here. I need you to trust in that and leave the rest alone."

"I would if I could," he said, laying his hand over hers. "Not only is this my job, but it's not in my personality to just have faith in people. I usually see the worst side of both humans and shifters."

"I understand," she whispered. Annabelle wasn't certain what that meant for the two of them, though.

"Can we put all of that on the back burner for now?" he asked. "I'll do my job to the best of my ability. You can keep your secrets for the time being. As long as you don't hinder my investigation, of course."

The words that Mac had murmured in her ears before he'd left her alone with Logan popped into her head. *'Give him a chance,'* Mac had told her. As scary as it was to take a chance, Annabelle really wanted to. "Yes."

A simple one-word answer. She hoped it was enough for him.

Logan leaned forward, brushing his lips lightly against hers. She sucked in a breath, then he pressed harder. The kiss was all-consuming as Annabelle opened her mouth and he thrust his tongue deep.

She tasted the hops from his beer mixed in with a smoky spice. Annabelle couldn't place the flavor and also had to have more. Gripping his shoulders to anchor herself, she scooted to the edge of her stool.

Logan slid his hands up her legs until he was gripping her hips. It was too easy to let him take her weight and lift her so she straddled his lap.

His hard erection grazed her. She wanted to feel more, though. Annabelle rocked while he continued to plunder her mouth. Was it hot in there or was she going up in flames? She couldn't tell.

"Baby," he murmured after he'd moved his lips from hers.

"More," she pleaded.

Logan immediately kissed her again, but this time he didn't thrust his tongue inside. Instead he nibbled at her bottom lip before swiping his tongue over the light bite. Annabelle found herself moaning and clutching at him.

"I'd like nothing more than to pick you up and find the closest flat surface to be able to feast on you," he said.

"I hear a but coming," she managed.

Logan smiled sweetly. "This isn't a one-night stand. I'm going to prove that you can trust me."

Annabelle dropped her forehead onto his shoulder as she tried to regain control. If just a little contact made her feel this way, how was she going to survive when he did finally make love to her?

"I want to take you on a date," he said suddenly.

She lifted her head and frowned at him. Had she ever gone on a date? Well, no—she'd met guys at the bar and let the conversation carry them to the next step.

"What?" he asked.

There was no way she'd admit to merely sleeping with guys who came through.

"Jesus," he said. "Don't tell me you've never been on a date before."

Embarrassment flooded her and she prayed she wasn't blushing.

"Damn, men have not treated you right."

She'd never thought to want more than what she'd always gotten.

"I will," he promised. Logan gripped her chin gently. "I will."

"Okay." She couldn't speak above a whisper.

Logan grinned, which made her smile at him in return. The childlike glee on his face was intoxicating. "Okay."

Annabelle ran her hands across his shoulders as she backed off Logan's lap. She stood between his legs, just looking him over. If she didn't walk away, she might beg him to fuck her. Logan was right to put the brakes on for the night. She needed time to think. A few hours ago, she'd been trying to figure out how to stay away from him. Hell, she had a file in her bedroom that would probably get her into a lot of trouble. Things were moving too quickly.

"I can see you're already starting to worry," Logan said.

"Yeah," Annabelle agreed.

"That's not always a bad thing."

"I don't know. Can I get back to you on that?"

He laughed. "Sure."

She stepped away. "You should probably get on the road."

"Actually," he said. "I'll be staying."

What the hell does that mean? "Staying?"

"Mac said he'd put me up for the night," Logan answered. "Trent took my bag to Calvin's old room."

Mac's letting Logan stay at the bar? He never does that. What if the alarm goes off or someone shows up out of nowhere? "Oh." She didn't know how else to respond.

"Is that a problem?" he asked. "I don't have to stay."

He sounded like he really meant it. "No," she told him. "If it's okay with Mac then it's fine with me." It was just really weird.

"You don't sound sure," he said. "If it's a problem, I'll go."

Did she want him to go? No, the answer was more than obvious. "Stay," she said.

"All right." Logan took her hand before bringing it to his mouth. He kissed her fingers. "You want to show me to my room?"

That was a terrible idea. There was a bed in there.

"I promise not to pull you inside and ravish you," he teased.

"Shame," she murmured then yanked him off his seat.

"Come on. I need to sleep if you're not going to keep me up all night."

"Tempting. I'll take breakfast with you instead, though. Then, tomorrow night, I hope I can convince you to spend some time with me away from here."

She'd probably be able to get Kelly to cover her shift if they wanted to sneak away before closing. "I might let you talk me into it. We'll have to see."

That infectious grin again. "We *will* see."

There was no one in the kitchen as they passed through. Mac was always the last one to bed. Even when he'd retired to his own room, he always got up and checked the locks before sleeping.

"This place is bigger than I thought," Logan commented.

Oh, he has no idea. "Yeah," she said instead. "Mac had to get a special permit for us to reside here, but since there's no hotel in town he was able to convince the town council."

"I noticed the lack of lodging."

It was her turn to laugh. "There are not a lot of towns that are purely for shifters. No one here is out to the public, so we've managed to keep trouble out."

"You think there'd be trouble if you came out?" he asked.

"Haven't you seen it?" she responded.

"Yes," he admitted. "But I've also seen humans and shifters come together and live happily."

"That's nice if you can have that," she said.

"You don't like humans much, do you?"

His question surprised her. They'd reached the hall and she stopped. "What do you mean?"

"It's just a feeling I have. I didn't mean to offend you."

"You didn't." She shrugged off his concern. "I guess I don't. I haven't had good luck with humans, even with them not knowing what I am. If they had... I don't know if I would have survived."

He tugged her closer. "I'm sorry for that."

"It's no big deal," she lied. It'd hurt. All the times that she'd been rejected had stayed with her. If the humans couldn't love her when she'd been a child needing them, then why would they be kinder to her now?

"Your room is the third on the right." She pointed just ahead.

"And yours?" he asked, seduction lacing his words.

Wow, I want to hear him talk like that in bed. "Last door on the left. Mac's is across from mine."

"That a warning?" he questioned.

"No," she said. "I'm a grown woman. But in case you need something, Trent is right beside you." She waved to the door before Mac's.

"I think I'll kiss you goodnight here, then."

She had to tilt her head to meet his gaze. He was several inches taller than her and that was hot. So were the muscles she'd felt under her palms earlier. Yeah, it was probably smarter to part here.

His hand was gentle as he cupped the side of her neck. "Sweet dreams," he murmured and brushed his mouth over hers.

Annabelle fisted the front of his shirt to hold him close, but he pulled away just as quickly.

"My control's not that good," he said.

She watched his toned bubble butt as he strode the few steps to his door. That had been disappointing. Annabelle waited until he was behind his closed door before she continued down the hall. She had a feeling that it would be all the thoughts whirling around in her head keeping her up instead of him. *What a pity.*

Logan leaned against the door to the room he'd been given as he clenched his fists. It shouldn't be so hard for him to let Annabelle go, but he was almost desperate for her.

This was so unlike him.

He didn't connect with people on this level and never so quickly. Logan had been partnered with Olivia for almost a year before he'd joked with and teased her. It came so naturally for him to want to make Annabelle laugh and smile. Logan was out of his depth.

He'd done the right thing. He knew he had, but Logan was tempted to go after her, so he needed to gather his wits. Pushing off the wood that kept him from making a huge mistake. He thenstalked to the bed. His bag sat on top of the dark-blue comforter and he dug around inside until he found a clean pair of underwear. He saw an attached bathroom and he realized that he needed a shower. The long day of walking around town then wandering in the woods was finally catching up with him. He was shocked that Annabelle hadn't run from him with the sweat scent coming off him.

The toiletry bag was at the bottom and, once he had it in his hand, he walked toward the shower.

There wasn't a whole lot of stuff in the bedroom. Calvin must have moved most everything in with Duffy. The nightstand was cleaned off, but there were a few knickknacks on the tall dresser he passed.

A few shells from a beach, a glass panther and some loose change. He shook his head. Logan was pretty sure he didn't even have that lying around. Even though he'd been in place for a few years, Logan never collected keepsakes. Nothing to tell others who he was. There weren't even any pictures of his friends or family. He wondered about Annabelle's personal space. Would he learn more about who she was if he saw her space? Or was Annabelle like him and kept herself hidden?

As he stepped inside the bathroom, he whistled. The bar might appear rundown, but he was realizing there was much more than what he'd first expected.

It looked like the entire space had recently been remodeled. The gray tiles on the floors matched what had been used on the walls. The room had no tub, but the standing shower stall seemed big enough to fit three or four full-sized men. Logan was excited to try the three shower heads he spotted. He went and turned on the taps to heat the water. He placed his toiletry bag on a hook then put his briefs on the counter.

Steam was already starting to fill the air and he loved it.

He undressed, making sure to slide his weapon under his jeans. It was within reach, but if someone walked in they wouldn't spot it right away. Logan didn't like leaving his gun out where anyone might see it, but he would also feel naked without it. His weapon felt as natural as wearing pants.

Condensation covered the mirror and he swiped his hand over it so he could stare at his reflection.

As beautiful as Annabelle was, he had to wonder what she saw in him.

There had to be tons of guys who came in and out of this place. She'd probably have her selection of men interested. Logan knew he wasn't ugly, but he also wasn't the most attractive male.

Maybe that worked in his favor, though.

Annabelle had obviously been dating the wrong type of guys. 'Dating' was definitely the wrong word, since she hadn't gotten to experience the rite of passage that came with going out with someone and learning about them.

Logan was going to change that. He'd make sure she got to make up for anything she'd missed out on.

That was something he'd be able to offer and hopefully it would give him extra points. He knew he was hard to deal with. His dominant side came so naturally that sometimes he spoke before he thought. Maybe he'd get some advice from Mac or Trent. They obviously cared deeply for her, so they might help him out.

Only time would tell, though.

Logan stuck his hand under the stream, hissing at the heat. *Okay, that might be a little too hot.* He adjusted the temperature until it felt right then stepped inside and closed the glass door behind him.

"Fuck," he muttered when his muscles began to loosen. He hadn't realized how stiff his shoulders were. *Speaking of stiff...* Logan pulled out his bodywash and poured some into his hand before grasping his cock.

He'd been hard for so long that if he didn't relieve some tension, he'd never be able to sleep.

The soap that he used had a clean, fresh scent that didn't bother his shifter senses. It also made great slick for when he needed to jack off. Which wasn't as often as he thought it should be.

The long hours exhausted him and, as he'd gotten older, Logan didn't indulge, because it seemed like he always had something else to do. He couldn't ignore his body's need tonight, though.

Logan ran his thumb along the thick vein under his shaft and pumped his hand faster. His member was already engorged and it wouldn't take him long to come. Leaning back against the warm tiles, he closed his eyes and remembered the feel of Annabelle on his lap earlier.

With those thin sweatpants she'd worn, she could have bucked up and rubbed until he'd brought them both to completion. He wanted so much more than that.

He wanted to know what she looked like swamped in pleasure so intense she grew dizzy. Flushed cheeks and bright eyes and gazing at him while he plunged into her soft body.

Logan tightened his grip slightly, drawing out his own satisfaction.

He could only imagine what it would feel like to be buried deep inside her.

Damn, he wanted to know what her inner muscles felt clamping down on his shaft while he claimed her as his own.

His climax hit fast. Before he knew it, Logan was panting and biting his lip to keep from shouting as his seed pulsed from his cock.

"God, yes," he whispered. Logan collapsed back against the tiles with shaking legs, barely able to keep himself up right.

That had been intense.

It was time to finish up and clean the day — including his orgasm — off.

He had a lot to accomplish, so he'd keep his promise of taking Annabelle out for the night. He wasn't certain of her schedule, but even if he had to think of a date activity for after her shift, he'd do it.

The aroma from the Italian restaurant had been marvelous, so maybe he'd get some takeout and they'd be able to picnic in the forest.

Annabelle had to enjoy the area if she'd gone for a run earlier. And wasn't she adorable in her feline form? He wanted to learn more about her species so he could shift with her one day.

Mac had mentioned that she might act like a house cat at times and he wondered if she had any toys that she enjoyed. When he'd been growing up, he'd had balls and a few fun items, but he had the feeling that Annabelle had missed out on that.

It couldn't have been easy growing up in foster care then around different species. If she didn't have anyone to enjoy the pleasure of being a feline with, Annabelle might not know just how much fun they could have.

Logan poured more bodywash into his hand so he could finish up his shower. Plans made, he now needed to get some sleep to prepare for the next day.

* * * *

Normally Annabelle didn't wake until after the noon hour and, since she'd tossed and turned most of the night, it was a surprise when she opened her eyes just after ten in the morning.

She was exhausted but also looking forward to the day.

Logan was probably asleep just down the hall from her. During the night, she hadn't been able to keep her mind from wandering to him. It had only taken a couple of hours from her deciding that she'd do whatever it took to keep him away to almost begging him to take her in bed.

So what in the hell does that say about me?

She wasn't in desperate need of companionship. Finding men to spend time with had never been an issue for her, even if it had merely been a drink and conversation that she wanted. Now, in the span of a few days, she felt like a different person. It was more than a little scary when she stopped and thought about it.

So maybe she shouldn't think about Logan? Or else she needed to think a lot more on the subject? *Shit, here I am going on and on again.*

Annabelle wasn't a fickle person. She couldn't be, with the life that she lived. There were a lot of people who depended on her. But Logan had made her question so much. Like never having gone on a date.

In the light of day, she felt foolish in having let him find out that secret. Did that make her sound like a slut? She hadn't really slept around, but it might seem like it to him. It bothered her more than it should have that he'd think badly of her. Annabelle wanted to impress him. At least until he knew her better.

Eventually, Logan would realize that she was neurotic and weird. Annabelle enjoyed shifting into her cat and playing as though she'd been born that way. Even her room showed her passion for her other form.

Mac had placed ledges all around the wall at different levels, giving her the chance to leap from one to another. She also kept a trunk full of cat toys under her bed. Even she knew that made her unique in feline circles. Trent was a panther and he never had the urge to paw a ball across the room so he could chase it. Just another way she was unlike every other feline around her.

Logan was a lion and, by the power that radiated from him, she'd bet he was one of the most dominant men she'd ever met. He was right up there with Mac and Magnus. It was a complete turn-on for her, but with the attraction came the worry that if she didn't watch it, she'd find herself in a situation that wasn't good.

Too many times, Annabelle had seen how a more dominant shifter treated the person they should have been cherishing. She wasn't about to let that happen to her. Or at least she'd never thought she would, but now Annabelle wasn't so certain.

Did craving Logan's strength and control mean she was weaker than she'd thought? Fuck, too many questions and she was tired.

Giving up on sorting out her confused thoughts, Annabelle rolled out of bed, literally, and looked into the mirror across from her. She appeared as worn out as she felt. Coffee — she definitely needed some caffeine to face the day. If she snuck into the kitchen now, she'd probably avoid nearly everyone else. None of them were what someone might consider morning people. Breakfast usually took place about one in the afternoon, so there was plenty of time before her family began to move around.

Still in the sweats and T-shirt she'd dressed in after her shower the previous night, she walked leisurely into the bathroom to take care of her morning routine. After, she made herself presentable enough in case she ran into any of her family. Carter was the only one likely to be awake and he'd no doubt have his head buried in a tech magazine as usual.

She quietly opened her bedroom door and glanced down the hall. There was no movement and Logan's door was still closed.

If she was really brave, she'd consider sneaking in and seeing if he slept in the nude. Maybe even crawling in underneath the sheets. But Annabelle wasn't ready to make that kind of move yet.

Annabelle slipped into the hall, making sure she shut the door quietly behind her.

As she passed the room Logan had been given, she slowed just in case he was moving around. Not that she heard anything. The soundproofing in the residence was pretty damn good.

Pushing down the disappointment, Annabelle headed toward the kitchen. She'd taken less than a dozen steps when she heard voices and laughter. That sounded like Duffy.

She sped up and practically jogged around the corner into the middle of the kitchen, then stopped suddenly.

Duffy was indeed home, and so was Calvin. But it was seeing them sitting at the long table with Carter and Logan that surprised her.

Duffy, Calvin and Logan were sitting together.

Panic flooded her and she didn't know what to do. Her first instinct was to back away and find Mac. This was bad, so bad, but none of the men seemed to share her concern. Just as she took a step to track down Mac, Logan lifted his head and grinned at her.

Caught, she waved awkwardly.

Logan's grin widened as Duffy barked out a laugh.

She glared at Duffy. Okay, that had been a stupid move, but she hadn't expected to walk into the kitchen and see all of them acting as though they were best buds.

"You okay?" Duffy asked, after he stopped laughing.

"Fine," she replied, trying to smile. Annabelle wiped her suddenly damp hands on her pants before walking to the coffee pot. "I just wasn't expecting anyone to be awake."

"We just got in," Calvin informed her.

"I was here first," Carter mumbled.

Duffy laughed at his best friend before slapping Carter on the back. "You know you missed me."

Logan didn't say anything, but he did watch her as she pulled a mug out of the cabinet then added sugar and creamer. Her hand wasn't entirely steady when she poured the brewed coffee into her cup. Annabelle took her time stirring her mixture, trying to decide her next move.

She'd thought she would have more time before she had to talk to Logan.

"Are you going to join us?" Duffy called to her.

If Logan hadn't been sitting next to him, Annabelle would have thrown something at his head. *What the hell is Duffy up to? Does he even know Logan's an agent and investigating him?*

"I don't know," she said. "When's the last time you showered?"

"Funny," Duffy replied. "I'll have you know my man put me up in a very nice hotel in Vegas. Had the softest bed I've ever slept in."

They hadn't been in Las Vegas, so at least she was getting his cover story.

"It was probably covered in fleas and no doubt you've brought them home with you," Annabelle said.

Logan snorted, coughed, before chuckling low.

"I don't have fleas," Duffy grumbled. "Pretty sure that's a dog or cat thing."

She turned to lean against the counter and lifted an eyebrow. "Want to bet?"

"You see?" Duffy asked Logan. "You see how mean she is to me? I don't know I put up with her."

"I'm pretty sure it's the other way around, honey," Calvin said, patting Duffy's back. The ten-year age difference didn't usually seem so big, but, looking at their worn, dusty appearances, Calvin appeared much rougher than Duffy. They'd have to have driven for days to drop Samantha off and return so quickly. It would have made more sense for them to have taken their time and not rushed home. Mac should have warned them away.

"You're lucky I love you," Duffy told Calvin. "You always take her side."

"Of course I do," Calvin agreed.

"Smart ass," Duffy teased.

Well, he'd managed to make her smile while relaxing her. Annabelle pushed off the counter and walked to join the men. Carter was farthest from her at the opposite end of the table, with Duffy and Calvin sitting on one side, leaving Logan and the chair beside him empty.

Annabelle slid into her seat and noticed Logan's mug was

about three-quarters full. Maybe he hadn't been there long.

"The coffee should be fresh," Logan said. "Carter and I finished off the first pot so I just made that one."

Duffy and Calvin both had bottles of water in front of them, telling her that they'd be heading to bed soon.

She knew the routine of her family, but Logan's she had no idea about. "Been up long?"

"Yeah," he said leaning toward her. "I have been."

Duffy slapped the table while chortling as she blushed at Logan's words.

"Okay, funny guy," Calvin said, standing and pulling Duffy to his feet. "It's time for bed."

"That's what he said," Duffy joked.

Carter groaned and Annabelle shook her head.

"You'll have to excuse him, Agent," Calvin said to Logan. "He's delirious from lack of sleep."

"That's—"

Calvin slapped his hand over Duffy's mouth before he'd finished his sentence.

"It's fine," Logan assured Calvin. "If you don't mind giving me a call so we can discuss that other business, I would appreciate it."

"As soon as we wake up and eat, I'll do that," Calvin said. He nodded at Logan before pushing Duffy into motion ahead of him.

"I've got work to do," Carter stated, rising as well.

Annabelle wanted to object at suddenly finding herself alone with Logan, but Logan placed a hand on her thigh and she remained quiet.

After Carter had left the room, Logan removed his hand and wrapped it around his mug. "You looked like you were about to bolt."

"I was considering it," Annabelle admitted.

"Regretting last night?" he asked.

She had to think about her answer. "Yes and no," she said.

Logan grunted. "Want to elaborate?"

How to say the words? "I'm not usually in need of saving. I don't want you to think I'm…"

"What?" he pressed.

"Weak." She whispered the word.

"No," he said. "That's the last word I'd use to describe you."

"Really? Then how would you describe me?"

"Strong, independent, smart, resourceful."

"You don't even know me," she responded.

"I should probably confess that as part of my investigation I gathered Intel on all of you that live here."

"Oh." She wasn't really surprised. Mac had prepared all of them in case they ever got questioned by the cops. There hadn't been any talk about the Coalition, but the same principle applied. She also knew what her file said about her. Mac had once given her a copy.

"Since you all did the same, I hope you're not upset."

"What?" *Oh shit, oh shit, oh shit.* How had he found out?

Logan chuckled. "Carter told me. He said it was part of his job to check out anyone nosing around the town."

"He does take his job seriously," she hedged.

"Carter also said he gave you the file."

"Why would he tell you that?"

"I asked," Logan answered. "He tried to stammer out something but ended up just admitting to it."

"Okay," she said. "So, are you mad?"

He shook his head. "No, I would have done the same thing in your guy's shoes. I'm a Coalition agent who shows up and starts asking questions. It's obvious that you all have a good life here and aren't keen on letting anyone in."

"I wouldn't say that. We're not exclusive on purpose," she corrected. "There are just not a lot of shifters who want to hang out in a territory with so many species. Some can't handle it."

"It's a unique situation, but it seems to work."

Annabelle rolled the tension from her shoulders. "It does."

"So I'll make you a deal," he said.

Why does that sound dirty? "I'm listening."

"You keep our date for the night and I'll forget about that file you shouldn't have."

That was a pretty good deal. Carter knew better than to admit anything to Logan, so she'd have to find out why he had. The young shifter lied for a living and could have covered them better.

"I think Kelly will work for me," she said. "What time?"

"Seven?"

"Okay," she agreed. That gave her all day and most of the evening to freak out.

"I have an appointment with the sheriff I need to get to," Logan stated. He pushed his mug away and stood.

"The hunters?" she asked.

"Yes." Logan gripped her chin and tilted her head back, just gazing into her eyes for several long moments.

"What?" she questioned nervously.

"You're beautiful," he told her. But he didn't give her time to respond before he lowered his mouth to hers. The kiss was soft and quick but still sent a zing of arousal through her.

"Uh," she managed after he separated from her.

"And, Annabelle...?"

"Yes?"

"Your coffee's gone cold."

Chapter Six

Logan pulled in front of the Brookside sheriff's department and let his truck idle as he looked through the blinds to see inside the small station. He spotted Magnus standing at a desk with a phone up to his ear and two other deputies working on computers.

It was a tiny place and he wasn't sure what to think about that.

Either Brookside didn't need a big law enforcement presence, or they were sorely underfunded. For Annabelle's sake, he hoped it was the first. He didn't like the idea of her having to deal with situations like the previous night if she didn't have proper assistance.

Magnus glanced his way and nodded through the window. Logan had placed a call to his office on the short drive there to have a couple of agents come pick up the hunter Magnus was holding in custody. They were due to arrive in about an hour and half, meaning he needed to get busy so he'd be ready to transfer them over. Logan hoped that after that, Magnus might have time to talk.

Seeing Duffy and Calvin this morning had really brought home that he needed to finish his investigating, even if his gut told him that Samantha was probably better off wherever she'd disappeared to. It was time for him to do his fucking job and not think about fucking.

He'd have time with Annabelle after he had resolved his case. There was no way that he wouldn't take the chance to get to know her better.

Logan turned the key and shut off his truck then pushed the door open. He gathered his laptop and files from the passenger seat then swung the door closed. Magnus had moved to the front of the building and waved him in as Logan approached.

"What's going on?" Logan asked.

"If you don't get that asshole out of my cell, I'm going to rip his throat out."

Oh wow, I didn't expect that answer. "What'd he do?"

Magnus ran his hands roughly across his face before he sighed. When he met Logan's gaze, Logan saw the anger the sheriff was barely keeping locked away. "He hasn't shut up all night. He keeps spouting off all kinds of hate." Magnus leaned closer to Logan. "Of course, my deputies are shifters and they don't deserve to have to listen to that shit."

"I agree. I didn't realize it would be so bad. He was actually pretty calm after we'd gotten the weapon away from him."

"He stayed that way until we locked him up. After he realized that everyone here was a shifter, he went ballistic. It's a good thing I separated his sons from him. The guy was losing his mind and might have hurt them."

"Are the boys still here?" Logan questioned.

"No," Magnus said. "Even though one of them was an adult and I could have charged both with illegal hunting, I allowed their mom to come pick them up. They don't need to be around their father right now."

"Good," Logan said. He didn't have a problem with the two younger men. It was the big bald guy who needed an attitude adjustment.

"You'll take him into Coalition custody?" Magnus asked. His hard stare dared Logan to say no.

Logan straightened his shoulders and looked Magnus in the eye. He would show no submission to the other shifter. It wasn't in his personality and Logan also had the added law enforcement connection. Most local police didn't like the federal government stepping on their toes. The power play could become strong between the two of them. "Yes, agents from my office are already on the way."

Magnus relaxed and grunted.

"That's what you want, right?" Logan checked.

"Yes," Magnus said. "I can't keep him long, so you take him and he'll be your problem. I don't want him back in Brookside ever again."

"I can't promise that," Logan admitted. "We work within the laws."

"You might not be able to promise that, but I'm going to make damn sure." Magnus stepped forward and pulled open the door, ushering Logan ahead of him. "Let's do this, then."

"You can't intimidate a suspect," Logan said quietly.

Magnus merely chuckled. "Who said anything about intimidating?"

Logan knew he was going to have to watch the sheriff. Not that he thought Magnus would break any laws, but he might not toe the line. Logan was a by-the-book agent. He would use every resource he had against the hunter, but he would not allow any of the guy's rights to be trampled on. "I'll handle him."

Instead of responding, Magnus led him to the small desk one of the deputies was seated at, working on a computer. The young officer glanced up at Logan and Logan had to keep himself from smiling. The deputy didn't look much above the legal age. He also visibly swallowed and grew nervous as he spotted Logan.

Taking a deep breath, Logan realized that the deputy was a coyote shifter. It made sense that the deputy would be wary of him. As a large predator, Logan's instincts would normally have him trying to intimate the weaker shifter. But Logan wasn't ruled by those instincts. Instead, he nodded at the coyote.

"Agent Logan Coldwell," Logan introduced. "I apologize you got stuck watching my suspect."

The coyote peered at Magnus before addressing Logan. "It was amusing at first, but all the name calling and threats got old real fast. I'm Deputy Carl Wilson." He held out his hand to Logan, which Logan quickly accepted and shook.

"I'll need to know exactly what he said. If he made threats against you for being shifters, I might be able to work in some charges for a hate crime of some sort."

Carl grinned. "I'll write my statement." He looked at Magnus. "With your approval, sir."

"Yes." Magnus patted the deputy on the shoulder. "Go ahead, Carl."

Magnus waved at the other deputy, who ambled over with a cup of coffee in his hand. While Carl had been young, fresh-faced and fit, this second deputy was Carl's complete opposite. With a beer gut, a receding hairline and many years on him, he didn't appear to be able to run down a two year old, much less any criminal. "This is Deputy James Garcia," Magnus said. "He was the one who actually got stuck with our guest all night."

"I apologize to you as well, then," Logan said.

James didn't offer his hand. He just nodded at Logan. "I prefer to work the overnight desk, so it's my own fault." James grinned, showing stained yellow teeth. "I might not move as fast as I did in my younger days, but I can still give as good as I get."

Logan nodded in acknowledgment. "My agents will get him out of your hair."

"No skin off my nose," James quipped. "It's usually empty here at night, so at least it kept me entertained. He fell asleep a couple of times and I might have accidently dropped things waking him up."

"Ah," Logan mused. James had gotten his revenge the only way he could and Logan approved.

"You want to talk to the guy?" Magnus asked.

"Yes," Logan confirmed. "I assume you ran his record for prior arrests."

Magnus snagged a file off the desk and passed it to Logan. Logan set his own stuff down on the corner before flipping open the cover of the folder.

Leslie Compton, aged fifty-six, married with two children. Worked as a machinist in a factory about thirty miles from Brookside. Leslie had a criminal background, which didn't surprise Logan, given Leslie's anger issues. He'd been arrested twice for driving under the influence and had spent time in jail for a couple of bar brawls. Yeah, Leslie was not the kind of person who Logan would ever want to be friends with.

"Great guy," he muttered sarcastically.

"You should have met his wife," Magnus said. "He screamed at her the entire time she was getting the boys. There wasn't anything she'd do, but he was cursing her for leaving him in. I'm more than a little worried about her when he gets out. I made a call to the local police down there."

"Any domestic calls?" Logan asked, although he had a feeling the answer was yes.

"Several called in by a neighbor, but the wife never pressed charges. Wife always denied that her husband abused her."

"Without any marks or a report, there's nothing they can do," Logan finished.

"Yep," Magnus confirmed.

"I'll pass that information on to my agents."

"While you're doing that, I'm going to call the officer I spoke with. When I told him you might be taking this guy in, they said they'd send a social worker over to talk to the wife. Maybe they'll be able to get her to understand the danger this time," Magnus said.

"I don't plan on letting him out anytime soon. He's a danger to shifters."

"Let's hope your agency agrees," Magnus commented. By his tone, it sounded like the sheriff had his doubts.

Logan would have to prove to yet another person in this town that the Coalition was there to help. *What is with these people?* "Where do you have him?"

"This way." Magnus jerked his head off to the side.

Logan snatched up his folders and laptop then followed Magnus down a narrow hall until they reached a locked door. Peering through, Logan saw Leslie sitting on a small bunk with his head back against the wall. Magnus unlocked the barrier and pushed it open before ushering Logan past. "I'll just leave you to it."

Magnus kept the door open as he walked away. Logan shook his head, but he had other things to worry about than the sheriff's mistrust. Logan sauntered forward until he was standing in front of the cell Leslie occupied.

"About time you showed up. You can't keep me here." Leslie rose, glowering at him.

"Actually, I can," Logan corrected. "You broke the law, and we're not talking about a fist fight with another drunk. You were hunting inside federally protected lands."

"So give me a fine and I'll pay it," Leslie said.

"Not going to happen," Logan said. "I have reason to believe you knew you were shooting at a shifter."

Leslie snorted. "Prove it."

"I will," Logan promised. "In the meantime, you're being transferred into the custody of the Shifter Coalition."

"I'm human," Leslie argued. "You have no jurisdiction over me."

"Wrong again." Logan walked up to the bars and wrapped his fingers around them. "You're looking at some serious charges this time."

"I know people," Leslie claimed, but he'd gone pale and Logan knew that Leslie was finally feeling some fear. It wasn't even a smidge of what Annabelle had felt the night before.

"You might know the pope and it wouldn't do you any good. We take attempted murder very seriously."

"Murder?" Leslie's face grew red as his anger spiked. "It was a fucking animal."

This was the problem. Unless Logan did something, this man was never going to see any shifter as an equal. *Fucking ridiculous.* Annabelle had every right to go for a run in a forest where she should be protected.

"And when I talk to your kids, are they going to think you were just after an animal?" Logan questioned. He already knew the answer. The teen from the previous night had given Logan an idea of what was really going on.

"You leave them out of this!" Leslie yelled.

"I wish I could," Logan lied. "You got them involved when you decided to take them into the woods in the middle of the night."

"I want a lawyer!" Leslie screamed.

Logan nodded seriously. "You need one."

He turned and walked back toward where Magnus had disappeared to. Logan couldn't question Leslie any longer until he had representation. That didn't matter, though. He was finished with him for the time being. He needed to write up his report and email it in.

Since he was working another case, Logan wouldn't have to follow Leslie back to town. Instead his office would handle the charges while he concentrated on what had first sent him into Brookside.

Logan knocked on the doorjamb to Magnus' office door. "Got a minute?" he asked.

"Sure." Magnus nodded toward a visitor's chair in front of him. "Have a seat."

"Thanks." Logan moved to sit.

"You get anything from him?" Magnus asked.

"No, but I didn't expect to."

"I figured," Magnus said.

"He asked for a lawyer."

"You going to call one for him?"

"They'll take care of that at headquarters," Logan replied. "It'll take a while to get him processed, so maybe he'll smarten up and lose the attitude."

"I doubt that," Magnus said.

"I agree," Logan admitted. "It won't matter, though. I was there and I know what happened."

"And you believe he'll get time?"

"Yes." Logan said with confidence. "The last case like this I was involved with didn't have half the evidence and the man was sentenced to fifteen years. The courts are taking these charges seriously."

"Finally," Magnus muttered.

"You don't believe in the system?" Logan asked, surprised.

"It's not that." Magnus leaned to glance out of his door and leaned forward. He braced his forearms on the desk as he spoke. "I tried to get Coalition help when your agency was first formed. We didn't have any trouble in town, but our town limit lines up to meet the federal land. I've been dealing with illegal hunting more and more."

"No one said anything about it last night," Logan said, growing concerned. He'd spoken to Mac and Annabelle and neither of them had mentioned trouble.

"They don't know," Magnus said. "I've been trying to keep it quiet."

"Why?" he couldn't help but ask. If Annabelle had had some warning, she might have taken better precautions prior to her run the previous night.

"The people who live here need the protection that we're able to provide. They depend on being able to remain unknown. If they start to fear hunters, or anything else, I have no idea how they'll react, but it won't be good."

The sheriff's words, said with passion, struck a chord with Logan. He could only imagine how Mac and the others at the bar would respond to a threat in their back yard. Logan didn't know the other residents of Brookside, but the way they had frozen him out the day before spoke of a close community.

"How can I help?" Logan asked.

Magnus furrowed his brow. "Help?"

"Protect the people of your town. You said that the Coalition hadn't assisted?"

"They haven't," Magnus confirmed. "I've made calls to them and the State Park Rangers. Still haven't seen anyone."

"My office would be the closest," Logan said. He hadn't

heard about any trouble up there. "Who'd you speak to?"

Magnus flipped through a notepad. "Agent Ruiz."

Huh, Ricardo Ruiz was one of the first agents who had joined Logan's division. They'd started about the same time, but Logan had never liked the other agent. "What's he say?"

"Not much. He promised to look into it and ask the Rangers to keep a better eye out, but I know he's just blowing me off."

"How many hunters?"

"This is the third time this month that we've brought someone in. I can't file the federal charges and without any help…" Magnus shrugged.

"You'll have it now," Logan vowed. He'd look into what Ruiz's issue was, but Logan had called in a couple of the newest agents and he doubted either would have a problem with getting more involved.

"Why are you offering to help when agents from your own office won't?"

"Because it's our fucking job," Logan snapped.

"Then I will expect you to do your job."

Even though Logan now understood some of the hostility coming from Magnus, it was hard not to feel challenged. "While we're talking about doing jobs, I have some questions for you."

Magnus lifted an eyebrow.

Logan opened his own file and pulled out the picture of Samantha Jones. "Have you ever seen this woman?" He slid the photo across the desk.

To his credit, Magnus picked up the image and studied it. "No. She's a pretty girl and I would have remembered her. Why?"

How much to tell him? Hell, Logan hanging around the bar had already showed Mac and his group that he was suspicious. Even if Magnus told Mac that Logan asked questions, it shouldn't come as a surprise. "We have a missing person report that links her to some of your residents."

Magnus leaned back in his chair and grinned. "Let me guess, your link is through the Den."

"Yes," Logan confirmed. "You know anything about what's going on there?"

"You seemed pretty comfortable yourself around them," Magnus replied. "What do you know?"

"Nothing," Logan admitted. "But I have my suspicions."

"All I'm at liberty to say is that if Mac or anyone in his group is involved, then that girl is in good hands."

Why didn't Magnus' confirmation that Samantha wasn't in danger there make Logan feel better? The sheriff knew something he wasn't saying and Logan wanted answers. "That's all you're at liberty to say?" he pressed. "You're a law enforcement officer. It is your job to stop a crime from being committed."

"I know what my duty is," Magnus replied, his shoulders going stiff. "I don't need a reminder from some uptight city boy."

"City boy?" Logan repeated. *Is he fucking serious?*

"It's obvious you don't belong here." Magnus ran his gaze down Logan's button-down shirt and dark slacks. "You'll get those nice clothes dirty."

Logan resisted running his palms along the thigh of his pants. They were tailored and fitted, but he wasn't wearing a full suit. *So I dress nicely. How is that a fault?* "I can't believe you're bringing up my clothes."

"It's only the most obvious sign that you're not from here."

"Your entire town has made it apparent that you don't welcome outsiders," Logan pointed out.

"For good reason," Magnus said.

Logan wasn't getting anywhere with this guy. It was frustrating him to a point that he almost threatened him, but by the look on his face, it seemed Magnus expected that reaction. Logan needed to be the bigger man here. "This case started by me doing a friend a favor."

"Favor?" Magnus asked dubiously.

"A buddy of mine got the call from Samantha's boyfriend, saying she'd been kidnapped by a couple of guys on bikes after they'd beaten him," Logan shared. "Samantha's not far from the head Coalition office in Lake Worth. The boyfriend, a sheriff by the way, got a look at the license plates on the bikes."

"Which led you here," Magnus said.

"Yes. He asked me to come up here since I was closer," Logan said.

Magnus tapped his finger on the desk as he stared at Logan. "What do you need in order to drop the investigation on this woman?

Finally, they were getting somewhere. "I want to talk to her. If she answers my questions over the phone, then I'll leave her alone."

"And leave town?" Magnus asked.

"I kind of like it here," Logan replied, not giving away his true feelings. Magnus didn't need to know anything about him and Annabelle.

"You stayed at the Den last night?" Magnus stated.

"I did." Logan gazed right back at the sheriff. "Is that a problem?"

"Not for me. Surprised is all. Mac is pretty protective over his people."

"I noticed."

"But him allowing you to hang around, even sleep there, says he trusts you," Magnus responded.

"I haven't given him any reason not to."

"Most people don't get the chance."

Logan nodded, not having anything more to say. He'd been surprised when Mac had offered. Even Annabelle had been shocked.

Outside the window, Logan saw a black, company-issued SUV pull up and park beside his truck. "My guys are here."

"Go ahead," Magnus said. "Carl has the transfer paperwork."

Logan hadn't had time to write his report. "Do you have somewhere I can sit and talk to them?"

Magnus pointed to the only other office, which was right next to his. "Use that space. No one else does."

"Thanks."

"Sure." Magnus glanced down at the photo of Samantha, which was still on his desk. "I'll work on this other matter."

Logan was grateful. He'd like to close this investigation up to concentrate on more personal matters. In the first time in his long career, Logan felt like he wasn't performing to the best of his ability at his job. It was not a feeling he wanted to carry around with him.

Fabian and Fredrick, twin wolf shifters, and Logan's favorite young agents, were stepping into the station as Logan exited Magnus' office. Fabian, a natural flirt and friendly guy, eyed and smiled at Carl. Fredrick rolled his eyes but followed his brother as Fabian walked right up to the deputy's desk.

"Well, hello there." Fabian's richly accented voice sounded warm and inviting.

Carl jumped up from his desk, knocking a few papers onto the ground. The young deputy blushed before bending to pick them up. Fabian made no attempt to hide his eyeballing of Carl's ass.

James snorted as Logan passed him, but didn't comment. The older deputy didn't seem disgusted or even bothered at all by Fabian's ogling.

"Hey, Logan," Fredrick greeted him.

"Thanks for making it here so fast," Logan replied, shaking Fredrick's hand.

"Oh, it was our pleasure," Fabian crooned, leaning against Carl's desk.

Carl looked like he didn't know whether to run away from Fabian or step toward him.

"Come on back," Logan said, hoping to keep Fabian on task while giving Carl a break from his intense attention.

"Be right there," Fabian said, turning his gaze to Carl.

Well, he'd tried. Fredrick followed him into the empty office. Logan switched on the light and was surprised by the clean, bare space he found. The space was about the same size as Magnus' and held a desk, a few spare chairs and filing cabinet.

"You made it here quicker than I thought," Logan commented, setting his stuff down.

"I lost a bet and had to let Fab drive."

Chuckling, Logan sat to power up his laptop. "You're never going to learn."

Fredrick grinned, sitting across from him. "If I let him drive, at least I don't have to worry about him playing with all the buttons in the car."

"True," Logan agreed. "Not a bad idea."

"So you said you caught a hunter?" Fredrick asked. "I can't believe he didn't know that there are no open areas around here. I looked it up before we left. This entire territory is protected."

"Oh, he knew. Have you ever heard anything about this place having trouble?"

"No," Fredrick confirmed. "Never heard of the place."

"The sheriff has made several requests to our office and hasn't received any help?"

Fredrick frowned. "Did he say who he spoke to?"

This was tricky ground. While Logan liked Fredrick and Fabian, he didn't know how close they were to Ruiz.

"It's probably that prick Ruiz."

Logan glanced up at Fabian, who was walking through the open doorway. "What makes you say that?"

"I've heard him answer calls. He'll promise to look into things, but I never actually see him working," Fabian replied. "When I asked him about the calls, he told me to mind my own business."

That wasn't good. Logan wished he could say something to defend a fellow agent, but he had a feeling that things with Ruiz were going to get worse.

"What else has he said to you?" Logan asked.

"Nothing I can't handle." Fabian clutched the back of the only other empty chair then spun in around to plop down.

"Like what?" Logan pressed.

"He calls him a fag," Fredrick supplied.

"Fred!" Fabian snapped at his brother.

"No." Logan held his hand up. "You don't have to put up with that bullshit. I need to know."

"It's not a big deal," Fabian said, shrugging. "I just ignore him."

"How many other people ignore him?"

Both Fabian and Fredrick looked uncomfortable.

"Never mind." Their reaction was enough. "I'll take care of it."

"We like working there," Fabian told him. "Not a lot of other divisions would have allowed us to work together."

"I understand," Logan said. He would make sure that whatever he had to do, nothing would come back on the twins. Logan opened the program he needed. "Let me explain what's going on and what I need you to do while I finish my report."

"Sounds good to me," Fabian replied, settling in to listen.

As Logan spoke, he outlined everything that he needed. Fabian and Fredrick both asked good questions, proving to Logan that they might be new, but they were highly trained. Once he'd given them everything he could, he stood and motioned them up.

"Let's get you guys on the road," Logan said.

"I don't know." Fabian looked out to the front. "Are you sure you don't need me here? I could stay."

Since Fabian was eyeing Carl, who watched Fabian from the corner of his eye, Logan knew exactly why Fabian had made the offer.

"Sorry." Logan slapped Fabian on the back. "But if something comes up, I'll give you a call."

"Figures," Fabian muttered. "I never get the good assignments."

"Deputies, can you help transfer the suspect to my guys?"

Logan called out.

"Sure." Carl was by Fabian's side in an instant. The shifter moved damn fast.

James grumbled but started to rise.

Amused, Logan turned to go back into the office and almost ran into Magnus.

"Here." Magnus passed him a piece of paper.

"What's this?" he asked.

"A phone number," Magnus replied.

Such a smartass. "Whose?"

"Call it and find out," Magnus told him before spinning on his heel and returning to his office.

Okay. Logan didn't follow the sheriff. Instead he pulled his cell from his back pocket and punched in the number while ambling to his computer.

"Hello?" The voice on the other end of the line was soft and trembled.

"Hi, this is Agent Coldwell with the Shifter Coalition," Logan said.

"Yes, Agent," she responded. "He said you'd be calling."

"He who? And who am I speaking to?"

"This is Samantha Jones."

There's no way it'll be this easy. "Samantha Jones?"

"Yes."

He scrambled to his file and opened it. "Samantha, can you verify your birthday for me?"

"April tenth, nineteen ninety-four."

"And the last four digits of your social security number?"

"Six three one one."

Holy shit, this really was Samantha. "Do you know why I need to speak to you?"

"Because I ran away," Samantha replied.

"I just need to make sure you're safe."

"I've never been as safe as I am right now."

Logan sat, not believing that he was actually getting to speak to the woman he'd been searching for.

"I won't tell you where I am," she said firmly.

"If I can verify your story and you feel that you are in no danger, there is no reason for you to."

She let out an audible long breath. "Where do I start?"

"Can you tell me what happened the night you left?"

Chapter Seven

Logan stepped into the Den and almost ran right into Mac. The big bear shifter laughed while moving to the side.

"You're back so soon, agent," Mac commented.

"Yes," Logan responded. "I am." There was no way Mac didn't know Annabelle had a date.

"I'm glad," Mac said. "I believe Annabelle is anxious for your date tonight."

Logan nodded.

"Or are you here about something else?" Mac didn't appear nervous in any way, but Logan was certain Mac knew about the phone call from earlier.

"I spoke to Samantha Jones today," Logan informed him.

"The young woman that you were looking for?" Mac asked. "I take it she's been found?"

"She states that she left of her own free will and that she doesn't want to return home."

"Isn't that what you believed?" Mac asked.

"It was one of the options I was interested in checking out."

"Then what's the problem?"

Logan glared at the biker. "You think you're pretty smart, don't you?"

"I have no idea what you mean," Mac said.

"Just because my case is closed doesn't mean I'm giving up on figuring out what is going on around here," he threatened. It probably wasn't the best move to declare his intentions, but he'd had all afternoon to think about what he was going to do.

After a phone call to Jamie officially took the Jones

investigation off his plate, he really didn't have a reason to hang around. Or at least that was what he'd thought before he'd asked Magnus for the records on all the hunting incidents that he'd been requesting assistance for.

Logan had believed he'd been grasping at straws for a reason to stay around until he'd actually read each report. Magnus did have a problem and it was getting worse.

"I have no doubt that you think you'll uncover something, but I assure you we're just a makeshift family who take care of one another." Mac shrugged.

"For Annabelle's sake, I hope that's true."

Mac's face changed. Gone was the cocky, relaxed man and he instantly hardened into the scary biker. He leaned close to Logan's face. "Don't think that because you spent a little with her that you know anything about what she needs."

"We both know there's more happening between me and Annabelle than hanging out a few times." Logan wasn't intimated. If Mac was testing him, then it was time for Logan to show him he was strong enough to be a true equal partner with Annabelle. If there was going to be trouble in Brookside, Logan wouldn't allow Annabelle to be involved. Her run-in with the hunters the night before was all she needed to deal with. She'd been lucky. "That's why you're letting me hang around, isn't it?"

Mac glared at him. "I'm beginning to regret my decision."

"No, you're not," Logan argued. "You're having a hard time letting go."

"So you think you know me now?" Mac practically growled the words.

"I've figured a few things out," Logan stated confidently. He was the one who stepped closer to Mac this time. Their chests were almost touching. "What I don't know, I hope you all will trust me with someday. What matters right now is that I'm not going away."

"Don't you have a job to do?" Mac questioned with a sneer. "A big bad agent shouldn't be wasting his time in our town."

"I do have a job to do," Logan confirmed. "I'm also entitled to a personal life." He relaxed his stance so that he wasn't directly challenging Mac, although he didn't put any space between them. "I care about her, and don't say that I barely know her. What I do know intrigues me, but it's the possibility of what we might mean to each other that matters right now."

"If you hurt her—"

"Then we'll cross that bridge when we get there," Logan finished. "It's possible she'll hurt me. That's the entire point of us getting to know each other."

"You're a cocky little shit," Mac accused.

"It seems to me that you're surrounded by cocky little shits," Logan quipped. "You should have plenty of room for me."

"I can't tell you anything until we know we can trust you," Mac said.

Finally, they were getting somewhere. "I'll accept that for now." Logan had no doubt that eventually Mac would open up. He had his suspicions about what was happening, but he'd give the shifter time.

"Is everything okay?" Annabelle asked.

Logan grinned at Mac before turning to Annabelle. "Hi."

She looked back and forth between him and Mac.

"It's fine," Mac said behind him. "I was just giving Logan the customary talk about treating you right."

Annabelle rolled her eyes. "I'm too old for you to be acting like some big old papa bear."

"Did you just call me old?" Mac asked, laughter mixed with his words.

"Well," she answered. "If the biker boots fit…"

Mac chuckled. "Fine. You two deserve each other."

Logan couldn't have agreed more. Annabelle had dressed simply in a pair of dark jeans and a low-cut red top. Her long black hair had a touch of curl to the ends as it flowed down her back. She was the opposite of every woman that he'd ever dated, but he felt like she was his match in every way.

"You look beautiful."

She placed her palm in his, allowing him to pull her forward. Logan threaded his free hand through her gorgeous, thick mane. It was just as soft as he'd thought it would be. With his hand buried at the base of her neck, he tugged her head back.

Annabelle shivered in his embrace. *What an exciting reaction.*

"Are you ready?" he asked.

"Yes," she whispered. "Where are we going?"

"I passed by the Italian restaurant on my way here. I thought we might have dinner there. If we can get in without a reservation."

She appeared amused. "I don't think that will be a problem."

Mac chuckled and slapped his shoulder. "I'll let Alexander know you're on the way." He walked off before Logan could ask him who this Alexander guy was.

"Alexander owns the restaurant and he's Mac's best friend," Annabelle told him. "Alex always keeps a table open for us."

"The guy that he and Duffy stayed with when they first came to town?" Logan remembered the story now.

Annabelle had been stepping out of his arms, but she stopped and stared up at him. "Mac told you?"

"Yeah, last night."

"He doesn't usually share about how he ended up here," Annabelle said. "You keep surprising me."

That was what he wanted to continue to do. "Good."

Logan wrapped his arm around her waist and moved her forward. "I think Mac likes me."

Her laugh was bright and surprised. Logan pulled open the door but didn't miss the happy smile on her face as she passed through first.

"He doesn't like anyone," Annabelle replied.

"I disagree. He was just waiting for me to show up so he could like me."

Outside, in front of the bar, the parking lot was well lit. There weren't any houses or other businesses in the immediate vicinity, so the tall street lamps and numerous security lights mounted were providing all the illumination.

"I don't remember it being so bright," he commented as he hit the key fob for his truck. He walked Annabelle to the passenger side before opening the door. She had to use the running boards to get inside. He enjoyed the way her pants tightened over her ass while climbing up.

"Mac had Carter and Calvin install some more. He's seen more activity in town and going toward the forest. He wants any strangers to know we're here."

"Avoid a run-in like last night?" he asked.

"We don't get a lot of problems, but it's possible. The new laws on hunting seem like a good idea, but Mac thinks that it's just going to push more dangerous situations like the illegal hunting."

It was a valid concern. He wished he could tell Annabelle he'd already started looking into the problem. Logan had spoken with a supervisor with the Parks Service and learned that Ruiz had told him he'd looked into the situation with Brookside and hadn't found any truth to the allegations. Logan wasn't sure what Ruiz was up to, but he'd be taking care of the agent in the morning.

In the meantime, the Park Ranger had promised to make his staff more available to Magnus. He'd even called the station before Logan had left for the night. Magnus had been pleasantly surprised and even wished Logan good luck on his date as Logan had pushed out of the door.

"That seems like a smart plan," Logan said, bringing his attention to the conversation.

Once Annabelle was settled comfortably in her seat, he leaned forward and kissed her cheek. "We're going to have a good time tonight."

She smiled. "I'm a little nervous."

"Why?"

"First date and all," she admitted. "I don't know what to do."

Logan placed his hand on her knee. "Just be yourself. I've made it pretty obvious that I'm interested. I want to have a nice meal with you, maybe take a walk in the woods you love so much, and talk."

"Just talk?" she asked. "Because I can think of more exciting things you could do with your mouth."

The little minx. Logan had been half hard when he'd walked into the bar, but now he was growing fully erect. "Yeah." He pressed his leg against hers. "We'll get to that later."

She shuddered. The evening was cooling down, but he knew she wasn't cold. Logan slid his hand up her leg to the junction between her thigh and pelvis. She sucked in a breath.

"We'll definitely get to that."

"Now?" He breathed out the words.

Logan kissed her. He'd meant to just tease her lips with his, but when he brought his mouth close to hers, Annabelle closed the distance, pressing them together. She clutched at the back of his neck while opening for his tongue.

One of them moaned—he wasn't sure who—and Logan pulled her sideways in the seat so he could fit his body between her legs.

He loved the taste of her, but especially when she let go, allowing him to ravish her. Annabelle tipped her head back, giving him better access. Logan brushed his fingers over her pussy, pressing down harder when she bucked against his hand. The scent of her arousal began to fill his head and he had to yank himself away or risk losing control. Even his lion was on the edge and anxious to claim her.

"We can't do this here," he stated.

A look of disappointment flashed over her features, but she nodded. "We should get to the diner before we put on a show for the cameras."

"Cameras?" he repeated stupidly. He'd known they were there, but Annabelle made him forget everything else around him. "Damn it."

She laughed. "You get used to them."

"Are there cameras inside as well?" he questioned, straightening his clothes to buy himself time to regain his composure.

"You mean did they capture me climbing into your lap and practically humping you?" she teased. "Yes, they did."

Jesus, he was lucky Annabelle wasn't pissed off that he kept putting her in compromising positions.

"It's okay," Annabelle assured him. "Like I said, you forget about them. We have an unspoken agreement that if we see anything that we weren't supposed to, then we don't bring it up."

"So this happens a lot?" Logan felt less desperate and could probably walk around the side of his truck without injuring his hard shaft.

"Have you met Duffy?" she asked with a laugh. "He's not exactly one to think about where he is before jumping Calvin."

Logan chuckled along with her. "I can picture that."

"Calvin's pretty good about getting them to privacy, but he says his will is only so strong, so there have been times we've had to turn off one of the monitors."

"I promise no one will have to turn anything off around us," Logan said.

She titled her head and studied him. "I think I'll enjoy getting you to break that vow."

Shaking his head, he motioned for Annabelle to settle back before closing the door. He sauntered around the front of his truck so he'd be able to keep an eye on her. Not that he expected to be attacked while in the parking lot, but he enjoyed knowing she was safe with him. He also needed a minute to himself, since his cock throbbed behind his zipper. He could literally picture bending Annabelle across the bar counter inside and pounding into her.

That was not an image he needed to take with him to dinner.

When he pulled open the driver's-side door, Annabelle sat grinning.

"You know exactly what you do to me," he accused.

"I like sex. I don't believe I should be ashamed of it."

"No," he agreed quickly. "You have nothing to be ashamed about." Logan was more intrigued. They'd have a lot of fun together. Maybe try some things that he had only dreamed about. He wondered how she would respond to his dominant streak.

With humans, Logan had to be extremely careful not to injure the women. His hold could become too firm or his partner might not be able to take the pace he'd reach if he let himself go. It was better with another shifter, but then the dynamics of their species came into play. As a large predator, Logan didn't find it easy to trust and let go, even in bed. It was one of the reasons he hadn't had sex in so long. He'd gotten tired of the disappointment after having to hold his instincts back.

He stuck the key into the ignition and started up the vehicle.

"I like your truck," she said, running her hand over the dash. "I expected you to drive a boring black SUV."

"We have those. But I prefer having my own ride. The company-issued vehicles get swapped around and I don't like smelling the other shifters in a car I'm driving."

"I never thought about it like that. I can see your point."

"Do you drive?" He hadn't seen anything other than bikes.

"I can," she answered. "I have my license for a motor vehicle and a motorcycle. I don't usually since I don't leave town and everything is within walking distance."

"What do you mean you don't leave town?" Logan put his truck in gear and eased out of his spot. The main road that would take them into town was a smooth blacktop, not the dirt road he'd first expected.

Annabelle fidgeted in her seat. "I don't leave Brookside."

"Why not?" he pressed. If they were going to keep seeing each other, they'd have to work out the logistics of the hour-long commute.

"I just don't."

Hell, of course things couldn't be easy. "Okay."

She snapped her head around to look at him. "Okay?"

"It will mean more driving for me, because I plan to see you as much as possible. Things would be easier if you'd spend some time at my place. On the weekends that I'm on call, I won't be able to come down, but we'll work something out."

"Just like that?" She sounded mad and he didn't know why.

"What?"

"This is our first date," she pointed out.

Logan slowed his speed as he came to Main Street. "Yes."

"What if you end up not liking me?" she asked. "We might be sitting in the restaurant and it dawns on you that I'm weird or something."

Unique, she was unique, but he didn't think that would help in this conversation. "What if *you* do?" he questioned instead.

"I don't know," she admitted.

"Exactly. It might not work out between us. But I have never felt as connected to someone as I do you, in such a short time. This is worth the risk for me."

From the corner of his eye, he saw her nod.

"The guys love to ride their bikes. I could always get one of them to take me to your place if it comes to it. I won't want to drive by myself and I really don't like cities, but staying at your place might work."

Logan reached over and grasped her hand, giving her a squeeze. "See, it'll be fine."

Annabelle was making an effort and he would do the same. Logan didn't mind coming to Brookside, though. Once Magnus had gotten over his distrust of Logan, he'd opened up a bit. The two deputies also ended up being pretty good guys. Carl had stammered and flushed a lot after Fabian had left, but eventually he'd settled down. James might not have been the sort of officer Logan would have preferred, but he'd ended up showing Logan exactly why Magnus kept him around. Not only had James remembered every detail of every case Logan wanted to discuss, but he'd also had several great suggestions on how to proceed.

Being impressed by the small sheriff station shouldn't have surprised him, but Logan had been happy when he'd left. If Annabelle was going to live in Brookside, she had a good, solid police force at her back.

That would make returning home a little more bearable for him.

There was a parking spot right in front of the restaurant, so Logan whipped his truck in.

"I guess you eat here a lot?" He'd wanted to take her somewhere nice and this place seemed to be the best in town.

"I love Alex's food," she said. "Kelly likes to cook for us, but when we can sneak out, we come here."

"Anything I need to know about the guy?"

"What do you mean?" She unsnapped her seatbelt before turning toward him.

"I like to know what I'm getting into with shifters," Logan informed her. It was important to have his guard up. Too easily other shifters saw him as someone to challenge. Logan wasn't sure if it was only his job or if it happened to all lion shifters.

"Alexander is great," Annabelle said. "He doesn't have a Pack—he's a wolf shifter, but he keeps mostly to himself. He and Mac became best friends, so we're able to get him out of the kitchen sometimes, but he still doesn't come around a lot."

"A lone wolf," Logan commented. It was rare for a wolf shifter not to surround himself with family or a pack. Fabian and Fredrick were very close to their pack and returned home every weekend that they weren't on call.

Logan envied wolf shifters for the fact that they always had someone they could lean on. His own family had easily turned their backs on him when he'd decided to go into law enforcement. They'd acted like he'd betrayed them by wanting to help the world.

It probably had something to do with his parents' extensive criminal backgrounds, but Logan had never expected that they'd cut off all ties to him. If he'd been a wolf shifter, wouldn't his family have needed that bond? Instead, if he followed his instincts, he was supposed to be okay living a solitary life. Meeting Annabelle had opened his eyes that while he might have been rejected by his birth family, he had other options. Instead of keeping people at arm's length, he could have his own makeshift family, just like she had.

"You okay?" She touched his arm, sending a jolt of awareness through him.

Yeah, he might be able to learn a thing or two from Annabelle.

"I'm great," he told her. "How about I buy you dinner now?"

The food had been fantastic, the atmosphere perfect, Alex had been on his best behavior, but it was sitting across the romantic table for two from Logan that made this the best night of Annabelle's life.

If this was what dating was all about, she'd insist that he take her on more.

Now, as they walked hand in hand through the woods behind the bar, she was enjoying pointing out trees that she had made nests in.

"I Googled your species."

"Did you?" She was flattered that he'd put in the effort. "And what did you find out?"

"Not a whole lot," he admitted. "There are a couple of groups trying to record margay traits and behaviors, but there isn't a lot of information released."

"I know," she said. "I don't know much myself."

"You had no one to teach you?" He slowed and pulled her to a stop.

Close by lay a log big enough for them to sit on. With the wine from dinner along with the pasta she'd consumed, Annabelle felt comfortable and happy. She could share a little bit about herself. Duffy had told her before she'd left on her date that she was going to have to talk to Logan. She didn't know how much he wanted to know. There were some subjects, such as the underground group, that were off limits, but she'd tell him about her childhood.

Annabelle led Logan to the log and sat. He quickly dropped down beside her. "I don't remember my parents at all. Mac has a friend who was able to get a hold of my social services file, but even in that, the information is limited. I didn't even know I was a shifter until puberty. I just thought I was a freak."

"Damn," he said quietly, wrapping his arm around her shoulder. "That had to be rough."

"It was scary," she admitted. "I knew I was different than the other kids in my foster houses, but everyone around me was human. Nowadays, they place shifters with other shifter families, so it's easier, but back then no one knew what I was."

"I'm so sorry," he murmured.

"It ended up okay," she said. "I like my life here. I have a good job, people who've become my family and I'm happy. I don't want for anything at all." She paused. "Well, that's not true. It can still be lonely sometimes."

"I can understand that." He ran his free hand over Annabelle's knee. "My family disowned me when I joined the police academy. They weren't good people. I never had enough to eat or clean clothes. They spent all their money on booze and drugs."

"I'm sorry," she whispered. "I would have figured you came from an uptight rich family."

Logan chuckled bitterly. "Quite the opposite. The trailer stank and was covered in filth. As soon as I was able to get out, I did."

"Why'd you want to be a cop?" she asked. Annabelle was honestly curious. Maybe Duffy had a point about talking and getting to know Logan better. The more he shared, the safer she felt. Maybe she'd judged him too harshly and he wasn't the straight-edged agent she'd called him.

"Because no one helped me," he said.

"I don't know what you mean."

"We had cops in and out of our lives constantly. They'd come to the trailer to pick up my mom or dad on a warrant. They saw the conditions I lived in. A few even made comments about the filth, but not one of them reached out and offered me aid. As I got older, I realized that no one was going to help me if I didn't help myself. The police had written me off at age eight. They decided that I'd turn out exactly like my parents and didn't want to waste their time."

"Fuckers," Annabelle spat.

Logan's laugh was warm. "Yes, but it did spur me into making a life for myself. The police academy was good because it covered room and board during my training. I had nowhere to go and no one to help me. It was either that or the military, which I seriously considered, but I was worried about not being able to shift."

"So you became a cop," she stated. He must have been so afraid, leaving home and everything and everyone he knew behind. Annabelle had run, but she'd been shuffled from place to place and hadn't had a home until Mac had found her.

"I haven't regretted it a single day of my life, even though I wish my family would talk to me. I wanted to help them get clean, but the first time I went home after graduating, my dad attacked me and I almost didn't make it out."

Annabelle's stomach rolled. She could picture Logan, much younger, offering his parents help and how that would have been received. "How long has it been since you've gone back?"

"Two years," Logan said. "I don't know why I just can't let it go, but every couple of years I drive by the old place just to make sure they're still alive. They don't talk to me and I leave them alone."

She snuggled into his side. "I'm sorry that happened to you."

"It left me bitter for a really long time. I don't have a lot of friends and the few I do, I'm not close to. Then I came to this small little town and saw how every species of shifter had somehow come together and lived peacefully."

"Amazing," she said. "Right?"

"Unbelievable," he agreed. "I keep waiting to be challenged and try to stay prepared for an attack. I've had to fight my entire life. Even in the Coalition, we're constantly jockeying for position. It doesn't seem to stop. Not until I came here."

"So you can just be yourself," she suggested. She tried to keep the relief she felt out of her voice that Logan understood why she loved Brookside, that he was beginning to understand how special the place was.

"The funny thing is I keep catching myself acting the same way as I always do," Logan told her. "With Mac or Magnus. I expect them to challenge me and react. I pissed off Mac earlier by acting like a jackass."

She patted his chest. "He's used to it. We do have shifters that come through town, thinking they can take on the big bear shifter. It never works out for them."

"Tonight, I realized that I don't want to be that way anymore. What you've all made here is wonderful."

Annabelle tipped up her head and kissed his jaw. "I think you're already fitting in. You don't have to be perfect. God knows, none of us are. You just have to have a kind heart and accept that there might be someone bigger or badder than you."

"I hope I get the chance to try," he confessed.

Oh, that's sweet. "I have the feeling that you won't have to try as hard as you think you will." Learning so much about him made Annabelle want to offer him promises. She couldn't and that hurt.

Logan cupped her face. His eyes dilated and the scent of his arousal grew stronger. *Oh, how interesting.* She ran her palm down his chest, feeling the muscles twitch.

"Enough talking?" she teased. While she enjoyed getting to know Logan better, maybe it was time to move things along.

"I don't know," he responded. "I'm not ready to end the date yet. What will we do?"

She laughed while reaching up and grabbing the back of his head. "If you don't know, then I'll just have to show you." Annabelle forced Logan's mouth to hers and nipped his bottom lip before stroking her tongue over the spot.

He moaned, but she didn't stop. Instead she kneeled up to swing her leg across his lap and straddled his waist. Logan grasped her hips. He gripped her tightly, rocking her against him.

His hard cock brushed the seam of her pants. She wanted to get her hands on his shaft, but first she needed to see his body. Annabelle tugged at his shirt.

"You want to do this here?" he asked, after pulling away.

"I don't see why not. We have privacy here and don't have to worry about getting interrupted."

"Someone might be out here, though," he pointed out.

"Well, it would probably be a shifter, so they won't come closer unless they want to witness what we're doing. Does that thought bother you?" Annabelle didn't want to push him past his comfort zone, but she was turned on by the idea.

Logan grinned. "You want to be watched, baby?"

It sounded so dirty, coming from his mouth.

"What else are you into?" he asked. He slid his hand around her ass and squeezed.

"I don't know," she confessed. This was new territory for

her.

"Let's find out." Logan pushed her to stand in front of him while he remained on the log. "Will you kneel for me?"

Oh, yes. She dropped down. Her knees hit a pile of leaves, but she didn't care.

"Good girl," he praised, stroking her cheek.

Annabelle turned her head to kiss his palm. She liked this new and interesting side of Logan. He smiled then whipped his shirt off. He had a nice chest, which was a favorite part of hers to admire.

Logan tweaked his own nipple before looking at her. "Now your turn."

She wasted no time complying. After dropping her shirt to the ground, she unsnapped her bra and let it fall.

"Perfect," he said, cupping her breasts. "You fit right in my hands."

Desire coursed through her and she gasped.

"Hmm," he murmured. "Now our pants." Logan stood, unbuckled his belt and left it open before tugging at the clasp of his slacks. Without ceremony, he pushed his pants and underwear past his knees then moved his shirt to where he'd been sitting. When he sat back down, he was on top of his shirt. "Take the rest of your clothes completely off."

It took some maneuvering to finish undressing while remaining kneeling. She could have stood, but Annabelle like the position she found herself in. Once she was naked, Annabelle gazed up at him.

"Anyone might see you right now." Logan's voice was husky. "But they can't touch you."

"I don't want them to," she said.

"I know. And I wouldn't let anyone. You can trust me."

That sounded like heaven. She could give in to Logan and he was strong enough to keep them safe.

Logan grasped his cock then pumped himself a few times. "Do you want to taste me?"

"God, yes!"

"Come here, then," Logan placed his hand on the back

of her head as she lowered down to hover at the tip of his erection.

She took a deep breath, bringing the masculine scent of him to the front. It was fresh and mixed nicely with the aroma of nature that surrounded them.

"Lick."

Shit. She squirmed, so aroused that she couldn't hold still. Annabelle ran her tongue over the slit of his cock.

"Good girl."

Annabelle probably shouldn't love to hear those two words. She wanted to please him so much that she took the crown of his shaft and sucked deeply. Logan bucked up while grasping at the back of her hair. He threaded his fingers through until he could push his cock in farther.

She took every bit of him that she could. It wasn't enough, so she wrapped her hand around the base of his cock and stroked while going up and down.

His pre-cum was salty, bitter and tinged with a buttery flavor. Unique—she'd never had anyone like him before.

"I'm going to fuck your mouth," he warned.

Annabelle moaned in approval.

"You can take it," Logan said. "I won't hurt you." He held her in place and began moving his cock in and out of her faster and faster.

The tip of his shaft hit the back of her throat and she had to work at suppressing her gag reflex. She didn't mind, though. Even when moisture pooled in the corners of her eyes, she didn't want him to stop. This was the hottest, most erotic scene of her life. She fucking craved it.

"Stop!" Logan pulled his cock away and she almost fell forward, chasing after him with her mouth.

"No," she pleaded.

"I'm not going to come down your throat. I want to be inside your sweet pussy."

She whimpered.

"Stand up."

Struggling to her feet, she had to rest her hand on his

shoulder to stand on her shaky legs. Logan didn't help. Instead he slid his hand between her legs to brush his fingers between her folds. She was already wet and needy.

"Please," she begged. Her entire core ached and her clit pulsed.

"Lean against me," he ordered.

She wanted him to keep making demands of her. Her mind was clouding and thought becoming nearly impossible.

Logan speared two fingers inside her and she clutched at his shoulders to lean against his side. His mouth was at her breast. He sucked her nipple and Annabelle started to shake.

"So much..." There were too many feelings shooting through her.

"You can take it," Logan assured her. He was moving his fingers in and out with the same rhythm that he'd fucked her mouth. She rode his hand, not having the right amount of pressure to send her over the edge.

"More," she pleaded.

Logan stood, sliding his body against her, stepping behind her and urging her to lean forward. "Down," he said.

With her stomach over the shirt and her knees digging into the ground, she allowed Logan to position her. His thighs pressed against her back and he also lowered himself to the ground.

"Is it still just the two of us?" he whispered in her ear. "Or do you think someone is going to watch me claim you?"

She shook her head, unable to form words.

"It doesn't matter," Logan told her. "Because I'm coming inside you and I don't care who might be around."

Annabelle arched her back, which had his cock rubbing her ass cheek. That was what she wanted, too.

"Do I need a condom?" she asked her.

"What?" she panted. Why wasn't he inside her yet?

"We don't have to worry about diseases, but what about pregnancy?"

"Birth control," she managed. "On it."

"Then I'm going to come inside you. Leave my seed and mark you from the inside out."

She was going to go insane. "Do it."

Logan chuckled then kissed the back of her neck. As he pressed the head of his cock inside her he also ran his hand down her side. He flexed his hips, pushing his shaft deep before pulling out then thrusting back inside.

Annabelle dug her nails into the wood of the log under her. His cock was long and thick, filling her in a way that no man ever had before. The connection went deeper than just taking a cock inside her. The feline part of her wanted to take over and transform to enjoy the large male mounting her. Annabelle would remain human, though. Logan's cock felt too good to give up.

She wanted Logan to hold her down and make her take him deeper. As though he could hear her thoughts, Logan pressed his hand to the top of her back, pushing her down onto the log.

"Yes," she whispered, wriggling, liking that she couldn't break his touch.

"Take me," Logan panted, leaning over her.

Sweat dripped from his body to hers and Annabelle was surprised that the water drops didn't sizzle—they were making so much heat between them.

"I am," she promised. "I will."

He pounded into her. Not in a way that a human would have been able to manage. No, Logan was moving so quickly that she barely had time to match him thrust for thrust.

Beneath her, the log rocked back and forth. Annabelle had to tighten her hold to keep from collapsing as Logan plowed his hips forward. She would ache later, but in a good way. Right then, all she managed to do was beg for him to make her come. She needed the release, her orgasm climbing higher and higher.

One hard desperate thrust and Annabelle's body felt as if it was being ripped apart. She screamed as she experienced the most intense climax of her life. She shook, couldn't catch her breath and her vision even wavered. Holy shit, she was going to fly away.

"Yes. Let me hear you. I want everyone to hear how good I make you come."

She was still yelling. Spent, she started to fall forward, but Logan's arm around her waist kept her upright while he continued to move his cock in and out.

His pace was slower, but he remained hard as he didn't stop. "I'm going to come and I want you to know that it's me who's filling you. No one else will ever get the pleasure of knowing what it feels like to have your muscles clamp down on them. You're so tight, baby, so good."

"Yes," she hissed.

He howled, his mouth so close to her ear that it startled her, but he sang his release to the trees and the sound echoed around them.

"We've got to do that again," she said, after he stilled, completely wrung out.

"I still have my cock inside you and you want to do it again?" Logan teased.

He circled his hips, moving his shaft around. She moaned. Yeah, she was going to be sore later.

"I want to do it all the time," she confessed.

He nipped the side of her neck. "I'll see what I can do about that."

Annabelle giggled, the sound happy and at peace. "You sound sure of yourself."

"I know that I want to see more of you," he said.

"I'm pretty sure that you've seen every inch of me."

Logan groaned as he pulled out of her body. She tried to lower herself, but he turned her so he'd take her weight. "I might have missed an inch or two."

Annabelle yawned. "I guess you'll just have to do better next time."

He pinched her side, making her gasp and jerk. "Watch it. I might have to find a way to keep your mouth busy if you keep getting smart."

She licked her lips.

Damn — just that fast his cock stirred. He was too old to go again so soon, but maybe by the time they made it inside, he'd have recovered.

Chapter Eight

Logan managed to get both him and Annabelle re-dressed, but the way that she remained cuddled into him and refused to allow him any separation had made the chore last much longer than it should have.

"If you helped me, we could be making our way back to your room, where I'll try to keep my promise of staying buried in you," he scolded.

"Let's just live here," she murmured.

He'd never had anyone respond to him after sex like Annabelle had and he fucking loved it. She was sweet, sleepy and very handsy. "I bet your bed will be much more comfortable." He hadn't noticed the chill earlier, but now that he could think straight, Annabelle's skin was cold.

She sat on his lap as he leaned against the log that he would forever think of as theirs. He had the crazy urge to mark the damn thing with his claws and scent so that no other animal would come near. He might still do it, too.

The shirt he'd pulled on was rumpled, wrinkled and torn, but at least it protected him from the worst nip of cold. He kept his arms tight around Annabelle so she didn't shiver.

"Or I could tie you to your bed and have my way with you," he offered. He was testing her reaction, and when her breath caught and her heart sped up, he was extremely pleased.

"We could do that," she agreed.

They weren't going to do much more that night, but Logan already knew that he would be back soon. He had to return to his office in the morning to check on Fabian and Fredrick as well as take care of the issues he was finding out about Ruiz, but he was going to be putting the miles on his truck. "Let's stand first."

She moaned, trying to burrow closer to him.

Logan had to lift her off his lap and set her on her feet. It was a good thing that he had shifter strength, but she was not cooperating with him. It was good to know that he could turn the hard-edged woman into a little pussy cat. He chuckled at his thoughts, knowing if he spoke them out loud, he'd see her claws.

He climbed up and stretched his arms over his head before once again bringing Annabelle against his body.

"Can you stay the night?" she asked when they began walking toward the bar.

"Yes," he told her. Like he'd leave her after the experience they'd just shared. "I have to get on the road early to get to work on time, but you can sleep in."

"We don't usually get up until late anyway."

"I know." The stroll through the forest was amazing. He didn't hear any small animals in the area, but if he had been in his lion form he might have been able to track them down. Not that he caught his prey, but the chance was always fun.

They'd covered about half the distance to the Den when a gunshot cracked through the silent night.

"What the hell?" Annabelle perked up. "Was that a gunshot?"

"For a small quiet town, you guys are sure getting shot at a lot," he said.

"Mac!" Annabelle took off at a full run.

Logan was so unprepared that she was out of sight before he realized what had happened. Cursing, he took off after her.

He caught up quickly. Annabelle was fast, but she was also trying to remain quiet as she approached her home. Logan knew what she was doing because he was doing the same thing.

The back of the bar came into view and Annabelle dropped into a crouch. Logan joined her, peering through the branches to spot four large men surrounding Duffy, who was kneeling on the ground.

"Cal," Annabelle whispered, grabbing a hold of his sleeve.

Logan leaned forward to get a better look and spotted Calvin on the ground bleeding from a gash in his forehead.

"Where's Mac?" Logan murmured.

She shook her head.

A couple of the lights newly installed there had been broken. Glass littered the grass beside Duffy. The four men had to have ambushed Duffy and Calvin, but what did they want?

"Do you know who those men are?" he asked.

Again, she shook her head.

Logan couldn't hear what the man leaning over Duffy was saying. The tension in Duffy's body was obvious and Logan had the feeling that if he didn't do something quickly, Duffy wouldn't stay down for long. Not with Calvin laid out a few feet from him.

Duffy wouldn't be able to take on all four men.

"I'm going to go out there and try to talk to them," Logan whispered against her ear. "Can you go around the front and find Mac?"

"I'm not leaving you."

"They're not going to hurt me. I have a badge." He wished he had his gun, but he'd locked it inside his truck earlier. He hadn't expected to need it during his date, but now that he thought about it, maybe he needed to carry any time he was around this group.

"You don't know that," Annabelle said. "I'm not leaving any of you. Someone will spot what's happening on the cameras."

"Fuck," he spat. "Fine, then follow my lead."

He yanked Annabelle up by her arm before slinging his around her shoulder. He began walking awkwardly and clumsily out of the tree line.

"What are you doing?" she asked angrily.

"Just play along," he replied.

"You better not get us shot."

It was hard to hold back a smile. "Hey, baby," Logan called, making his voice show he'd been drinking heavily. "I think this place is open."

"Don't you think you've had enough to drink?" Annabelle said on cue.

"I'll tell you when I've had enough," he sputtered.

"Sorry." She dipped her head and sounded contrite, although they both knew she was far from it.

"Who's there?" The big guy gripped Duffy's shoulder, holding him in place.

"Hey, man," Logan slurred. "You still open? I need a beer."

The big guy relaxed and that was when Logan recognized him. Frank Nunez. Samantha's boyfriend. Damn it, he should have insisted that Annabelle went for help. She didn't react at all to the man, but the way that Duffy was growling while shaking with anger showed that this wasn't the first time he'd met Frank.

Samantha had told him that Duffy and Calvin had stopped Frank from beating her and dropped her off a couple of blocks from the restaurant where a friend lived. From there Samantha had taken off on her own.

Even though Logan had doubted some points in her story, she'd been safe and he had no reason to press her. Samantha was an adult who could come and go as she wanted. He had no business getting involved if she wasn't in any danger.

Now that Frank was standing in front of him, Logan wanted to show him that he wouldn't get away with beating a woman ever again.

"What's going on here?" Logan sing-songed.

"This isn't any of your business," Frank told him.

Calvin opened his eyes and slowly turned his head to Logan. Their gazes met and Calvin gave a small nod. It would be four against four. Even if Logan didn't want Annabelle involved, he didn't know if he could take two of the guys. Although he'd been trained for more than just regular police work, these were shifters he was up against.

"Move along." Frank pulled out his badge.

"Hey!" Logan sang, still acting. He lurched several feet, bringing him and Annabelle well within Frank's circle. "I have one of those, too." He slid his badge from his back pocket. "And look at that. It says Shifter Coalition agent, which trumps your sheriff's badge," he added, ice cold.

Frank looked confused then angry. "What is this?"

"I believe that's my question." Logan stalked closer until he faced Frank. "Now, drop any weapons you have."

Frank grinned. "What weapons?"

They both knew that not only was Frank carrying, but so were his men.

"As an agent of the Coalition, I demand you stand down," Logan ordered.

"You're all alone here, Agent," Frank said. "So I'm going to have to refuse." He motioned for one of his men to come forward. "We'll be finished with this man after he tells me what I want to know." Frank seized the top of Duffy's hair and yanked his head back.

At the same time, Duffy brought his arm up right between Frank's legs. The sound that Frank made as he dropped to his knees was pitiful. Calvin leaped to his feet and tackled the guy closest to him. Annabelle spun while kicking out and knocked the guy that Frank had sent toward them onto the ground. That only left the huge red mountain of a man.

With a series of kicks, punches and blocks Logan both drove the guy away from the group and protected his own body. The mountain man did deliver one good punch to Logan's ribs that knocked the breath out of his lungs, but Logan managed to place a well-aimed kick to the guy's sternum, making him fly back.

"What the fuck?"

The rear door flew open and Mac, Carter and another woman ran out.

Calvin had knocked his opponent unconscious and was

now leaning over Duffy, who sat on Frank's back. Carter and the unknown woman came to Annabelle's aid as Mac stalked toward him.

"Check Calvin," Logan told Mac. "He took a pretty bad knock on his head."

"I called the sheriff when I saw from the cameras what was going on," Carter said.

Mac turned toward Calvin. "You okay?"

"Yeah," Calvin said, his gaze still on Logan. "Two of them came up from behind and surprised me."

"Probably didn't help that I had my hand on your ass," Duffy muttered. "I'm sorry."

"Are you kidding?" Calvin turned to his partner and grabbed him. "I'm so proud of you. Did you see how fast that asshole fell when you hit him?"

"I heard your voice in my head telling me what to do," Duffy said to Calvin.

"I knew the training would pay off," Calvin praised. "But you're not the only one with training." With Duffy still against his chest, Calvin looked at Logan. "Nice move."

Logan nodded. He heard the suspicion in Calvin's tone.

"What are you talking about?" Annabelle asked, joining them. It appeared that Frank and his men were tied up, awaiting the sheriff.

"You want to tell them or do you want me to?" Calvin asked him.

Logan's gut clenched. He had a bad feeling. "Tell them what?"

"Where you got your training and what you do in your free time," Calvin said.

"Logan?" Annabelle ran her hand across his arm. "What's he talking about?"

"I have special training," Logan told her.

"Okay." She sounded confused.

"Calvin," Mac's voice held a warning.

"She has a right to know!" Calvin exclaimed.

"It's not your place," Mac said, but he turned a cold gaze

onto Logan. "I had no idea."

"It's not something I'm at liberty to discuss," Logan said stiffly. It was obvious that Annabelle had no idea what they were talking about, but Mac, Calvin, Duffy and Carter were all staring at him.

Magnus walked around the corner with Carl and Fabian. Logan frowned at his fellow agent.

"What are you doing here?" he asked Fabian when the younger man reached him.

"I was on a date with Carl when the sheriff called and said he needed him," Fabian said. "When I heard your name, I decided to tag along."

Having a friendly face there was a relief.

Fabian motioned toward the men, who Magnus was taking into custody. "It appears you've been keeping the sheriff's office here busy."

Logan glanced around the small yard and the people that he had gotten to know. More secrets. Calvin obviously knew exactly what Logan had been through and, by the sounds of it, he wasn't happy about it. The other men were also aware. The only conclusion that Logan could come up with was that Calvin had also been recruited for the black-ops missions Logan had carried out. It seemed he had more in common with these people than he'd realized.

"They seem to keep themselves busy around here," Logan told him.

"What do you need me to do?" Fabian asked. He didn't look like a Coalition agent at the moment. He wore red skinny jeans and a thin, shiny button-down shirt.

"You sure you want to work tonight?" Logan asked.

Fabian shrugged. "I've got the feeling that my date's going to be busy for the rest of the night. Might as well help you out."

Frank yelled and lunged at Magnus. Both Logan and Fabian started forward, but Magnus lifted Frank off his feet and slammed him to the ground. Everyone in the yard froze and Logan gaped at the sheriff.

Magnus straightened to his full height and glanced at Carl. "Let's take them in."

Carl nodded before turning to Fabian to give him a look of regret. Fabian grinned back and nodded.

"Go talk to him," Logan said. "Let me figure things out around here."

"Thanks." Fabian jogged to Carl as Logan walked toward Mac and his group.

"We all know why he was here," Logan said to the group. "Can we stop messing around and just tell the truth?"

Annabelle shifted from foot to foot while Calvin and Duffy glared at him.

"You guys go inside," Mac said. "We'll be right in."

Duffy clutched Calvin's arm and dragged him away while Carter followed. The woman from earlier had disappeared already.

"It's okay, Annabelle," Mac said. "I just need to make sure things out here are being taken care of."

"What am I not being told?" she demanded.

Mac shook his head. "Not here."

Annabelle jerked her head back like she'd been slapped.

Logan wanted to pull her into his arms but he didn't think she'd accept his touch. "Do not dismiss me."

"No!" Mac moved quickly until he stood in front of her. "What we have to say just can't be discussed outside the family."

"Fine." Annabelle whirled to Logan. "You better not have lied to me."

"I haven't lied," he assured her. "Everything I've told you is the pure truth."

She didn't look like she believed him.

"I swear to you," he said. "I may have left out some things about myself but I wouldn't outright lie."

"But I don't know you well enough to know if I can trust your word."

"It's not like we have had a lot of time to talk. We're still in the getting to know you part," Logan pointed out.

She nodded before turning toward the back door. Dread filled him. They'd had such a great night and now everything was getting screwed up.

"You did good protecting my family," Mac praised.

Logan wasn't usually one who needed compliments, but it felt good to know that he'd made Mac proud.

"I'm glad I was here, although they took care of themselves. Even Annabelle had no problem defending herself," Logan said.

"Everyone has some sort of self-defense training. Duffy has always struggled, but Calvin has been working with him more," Mac said. "In the world we live in, it's good to be prepared."

"I agree."

"Send your agent away and come inside and talk to us," Mac said.

"You'll tell me what's going on?" Logan pressed.

"Yes," Mac said, not hedging one bit. "But you need to think about what you're going to tell Annabelle about your other job. She doesn't know about Calvin, but if she starts questioning him, he'll tell her the truth."

"I'll think about it," Logan said. He waited until Mac walked through the open back door. Magnus was heading in his direction and the four suspects were gone.

"What are we holding them on?" Magnus questioned.

As Logan named several charges, he tried to gauge Magnus' mood.

"Anything else?" Magnus questioned.

"He's connected to the case that brought me here," Logan shared. "The one you put down was Samantha Jones' boyfriend."

"The man she was running from," Magnus stated.

"I also wouldn't be surprised if one of the others ends up being her brother."

"Her brother?"

Logan shook his head. "It's not good if her brother Mike is here. It wouldn't be to help her."

"I understand," Magnus said. "You'll be taking them into custody as well."

"Yes," Logan confirmed. "I'll be by in the morning to start the paperwork."

Magnus slapped him on the shoulder. "Maybe I should just let you have that extra office we have. You've been spending more time there than in your own."

Logan laughed. "I'll have to return to my own job eventually."

"Maybe," Magnus stated. "I guess we'll have to see."

Logan didn't know what Magnus meant, but it didn't matter. He needed to figure out what to say to Annabelle. His handler with Military Intelligence had warned him that he could never tell anyone about the missions he'd been called out on. Logan had hated them, but he was in too deep after years of service and couldn't see any way out. In fact, his handler had told him numerous times that he wouldn't be leaving the program.

It was the biggest mistake that he'd ever made, accepting the missions, but Logan had needed money and hadn't known any better. Now it seemed as though his past might keep him from Annabelle.

He was alone in the yard. Everyone had either gone inside or left with the sheriff. Logan couldn't put Annabelle off for long. At least he was finally getting some answers to his questions.

Instead of the cuddling and quiet evening with Annabelle, he might be headed home alone. He wouldn't be giving her up, though. If she needed time, that was one thing, but he wouldn't allow her to push him away. Sure, he'd made some mistakes, but he wasn't a bad guy.

Logan hurried to the rear entrance, trying to pull out the confidence he carried during his job. He would stand tall, listen and explain the best he could.

He walked down the quiet hallway to the kitchen. It had appeared to him that Mac, Annabelle and the others congregated there often.

The soft murmur of voices was all he heard when he reached the doorway. Mac and Annabelle sat at the table with mugs of coffee in front of him. Mac spotted him first and waved him in.

"We were just trying to warm up," Mac said. "Can I get you a cup?"

"Sure," Logan agreed.

Annabelle glanced up at him and she didn't seem mad. Concerned, anxious and maybe confused, but she did smile at him. Taking that as a good sign, he sat in the chair next to her.

"You okay?" he asked.

"Yeah." She nodded. "It seems like it's been days since we were in the woods."

"We should have stayed when you suggested it."

"It would have never worked. We wouldn't have had any coffee."

"Too true," he said with a laugh.

Mac rejoined them, passing Logan a steaming cup. The strong aroma rose and he leaned down to really enjoy it. Then he picked up the mug and sipped before looking at Mac and Annabelle. "Where do you want to start?"

Annabelle dropped her gaze onto the table as Mac patted her back.

"You've read my file," Mac said. It wasn't a question.

"Yes."

"So you know what happened to my sister?"

"I do."

"After I got custody of Duffy, I planned to take him away to a new life. I told you how we ended up here," Mac said. "What I left out was that the first woman I met, who worked for Alexander, was also an abused wife. Except she managed to get out before she got killed."

"That had to be rough," Logan said with sympathy.

"It was then I realized that it didn't matter how far I drove. The past would always be there. I liked this town and Alexander was kind to us. I didn't have much I could offer, but I could think of one way to repay Alexander's friendship."

"You found a way to protect the woman that worked for him," Logan guessed.

"Yes," Mac confirmed. "I still had contacts from the army and I was able to place her with a family of bobcats who she fit right in with."

"Your first placing," Logan stated.

"You knew?" Annabelle murmured.

"No," Logan shook his head. "Not until I started to put everything together today. After I spoke to Samantha, I knew someone from here had to be involved. A lot more involved than just driving her a few blocks to a friend's house."

"But you didn't press her for answers," Mac said.

"She was trying to protect you, to thank you for what you did for her. I wasn't going to make her betray that vow."

"I knew you'd catch on eventually," Mac said.

Logan shrugged. "I'm kind of embarrassed that it took me this long."

"I can't believe you figured it out at all," Annabelle said.

He turned toward her. "You're what I couldn't fit into the whole plan."

"Why me?" she asked.

"You lied to me. Said you never saw Samantha," he reminded her.

"I did." She didn't sound a bit sorry.

"I couldn't tell at the time what you were hiding," Logan admitted. "Not with any of you. And I never scented Samantha here."

"We use a neutralizer," Annabelle told him.

"And we've had years of practice making up cover stories," Mac added.

"I'm impressed." Logan gave them credit. "How many people have you helped?"

"Too many to count," Mac said. "We've been doing this a long time."

"Any problems?" Logan had to ask.

"Not until some do-good Coalition agent showed up," Mac said.

Logan laughed. "I hear he's a prick."

"I kind of like him," Annabelle stated.

"Me, too," Mac agreed.

"I'm not going to say anything to anyone," he promised. "I also won't interfere with your operations."

Annabelle gasped. He reached and captured her hand with his before bringing it to his lips.

"Did you think that I'd try to stop what you're doing?" he asked her.

She nodded, still appearing shocked. "You just seemed so strait-laced."

"Well..." Logan blushed. "That's not really how a man wishes to be described."

Annabelle smiled. "Apparently, I didn't mind strait-laced, stuffy or —"

"Okay, that's enough." Logan held up his hand. "I agreed to being somewhat rigid but that's it."

Her giggle warmed him and he found himself smiling, too. Then he remembered what else they needed to discuss.

"I have something else to tell you," he said.

"What?" She turned her palm before twining her fingers in his.

He looked at Mac, who nodded. "It will be okay," Mac told him.

"After I graduated from the police academy, I was approached by someone from the government who'd figured out what I was. In order to protect anyone from knowing about shifters I went to work for him."

"What kind of work?" she asked. Her hand didn't leave his, though. Instead she scooted her chair closer.

"They sent me and an entire group of shifters on missions that were labeled too dangerous for humans. We went to other countries. All around the world."

"What did they make you do?"

"Sometimes we rescued American citizens," Logan said. "But sometimes we took out the people who our government deemed the enemy."

"Oh." She bit her bottom lip. "I'm so sorry they made you do that."

"No," Logan corrected her. "I chose to join. I didn't know what the job would entail at the beginning and they offered me a lot of money. I wanted the money. I didn't do it out of some sense of loyalty to my country. I agreed because I didn't want to end up like my parents."

"It doesn't matter," she told him. With her free hand, she cupped his face. "You were just a kid and you didn't know what you were agreeing to." She looked at Mac. "Calvin is a part of this, too?"

"Yes," Mac confirmed. "He'll tell you his story if you ask, but it's hard for him to talk about. The missions he went on took a lot out of him. It was why he left the police force and how he ended up here."

"I don't need to know his story," she said. "If he wants to tell me someday, I'll listen, but it's enough that he's a part of us now."

Mac beamed at her with pride, but Logan still wasn't finished. "It's not done. Even if they haven't called on me in a while, it's always possible that they'll request me at a moment's notice."

"You're still in?" Mac asked in alarm.

"It's a forever commitment," Logan said. "There's no way out."

Mac grinned. "I wouldn't be so sure about that. Let me make some phone calls and I'll see what I can do."

Logan's pulse spiked as excitement zipped through him. "You might be able to get me out?"

"Yes." Mac nodded. "I've been trying to get the entire program shut down and hope that will be the eventual resolution."

Logan's mind spun. He couldn't believe this. "I want out," he said firmly. "I don't care what it takes."

Mac tapped his fingers on the table. "I'll take care of it."

Mac stood and Logan didn't feel right leaving it at that. Logan walked around and held out his hand.

"I don't know if I'll ever be able to thank you for this," Logan told him.

"You don't have to thank me," Mac said. "You never should have been placed in the situation to begin with." Mac shook Logan's hand. Before Logan could react, Mac then pulled him into a quick hug. "Now I suggest you both turn in. It's been an exciting night." Mac released him and Logan was embarrassed at how good the attention from Mac felt.

Logan held his hand out to Annabelle in order to help her to her feet. "Sounds like a good idea to me."

Annabelle wrapped her arm around his lower back and they walked out of the kitchen together while Mac headed into the main bar area. Logan hadn't even thought about the fact that the bar was still open. It wasn't closing time yet at just past midnight.

"You are sleeping in my room, right?" she asked.

"Of course," he said. "As long as that's where you want me."

"It is."

The walk down the hall had a completely different feel than it had last night. The previous evening had been filled with possibilities and nerves. Now, as he leisurely strolled with Annabelle by his side, Logan was more content and happy than anything else.

They'd gotten two big talks out of the way and that had taken a load off his chest. He'd taken a chance at discussing the missions, but he was glad he had. If Mac really could get him out of them, his entire life would change.

"You're thinking awfully hard," Annabelle commented.

"A lot has happened tonight," he replied.

"True." They reached her door and she opened it before ushering him inside. "This is it."

A black-framed bed dominated the room, catching his

eye. She had a black comforter over it, but he saw red sheets peeking out. There was a long dresser against the south wall with a mirror above. What really drew his attention were the ledges that seemed to float from the walls at several different heights. He'd call them shelves, but they didn't hold anything.

"Did you just clean up in here?" he asked.

"No, why?" She'd ambled toward the window to pull the black curtains closed but stopped to glance back at him.

He pointed to the closest ledge.

She blushed adorably.

"What?"

"I like to climb."

"We talked about that," he reminded her.

"I also like to jump," she said.

He thought he understood. "So you shift in here and play?"

"Yeah." She was obviously embarrassed.

"I think that's cute," he said.

"Cute?" she repeated.

"Next you'll tell me you have a toy box full of cat toys."

She actually shuffled her feet and looked away.

"Wow," Logan exclaimed. "That's awesome."

"Shower," she blurted out. "You should probably shower before bed."

Logan laughed then stalked across the room toward her. She backed away until her knees hit the bed. "I'm not making fun of you."

"It's okay. I know I'm weird."

"Not weird," he corrected. "Fun, refreshing and, yes, cute."

Her smile grew. "You really think so?"

"Yes, and do you know what else I think?"

"What?" she asked.

"That a shower sounds good," he said. "As long as you'll join me."

"Okay," she agreed quickly before grasping his hand and

towing him to one of the closed doors.

Her bathroom was very similar to the one in the guest room he'd stayed in previously, except hers was done in different shades of green. He liked it immediately. She also had a large claw-foot tub as well as a big shower stall.

"Bath or shower?" he asked.

"Shower tonight, I think," she replied. "I am kind of tired."

"You got it." He walked over and started the water. "Now let me see that beautiful body again."

Annabelle shut the bathroom door before undressing. Logan watched every move she made so he could appreciate each gorgeous inch of flesh.

It was obvious that she kept in shape. Her arms and calves were well-toned and her stomach flat, but she wasn't skinny. No—she was perfectly proportioned. He was a little nervous to get naked in front of her. He wasn't as built as Mac, Trent or Calvin.

"Your turn," she said, walking toward him.

Logan pulled his shirt over his head and her gaze went directly to his chest. She'd made comments about it and apparently she really did enjoy the look of him. Annabelle even licked her lips.

"Hurry," she murmured. "I can't wait to see you all wet."

Logan laughed and the anxious feeling evaporated. He finished a lot faster than he'd meant to, then Annabelle was pushing him inside the shower.

The hot water hit his chest. Annabelle purred, a not entirely human sound, as she pushed him against the white-tiled wall.

"Will you let me wash you?" she requested.

How can I turn down that offer? "Yes."

Annabelle picked up a bar of soap from the dish by his hip then lathered her hands. Logan leaned his head back and she started at his neck and worked her way down. She caressed every inch of him until his front was covered in suds and his cock was straining for release. She'd even washed his shaft and balls, which he'd loved.

"Under the stream," she ordered.

Logan moved to comply as Annabelle slipped behind him, where she began giving his back and ass the same treatment his front had received.

"Turn."

He spun around, his cock brushing against her stomach. "All done?"

"Nice and clean," she said.

"Good." He took the bar of soap from her and repeated everything she'd done for him. Except he'd pierced her with his fingers, drawing out her pleasure. He kept two digits buried deep while finishing, making her all slick from the inside out.

It wasn't hard to gauge how much she was enjoying his touch as her moans and gasps grew in volume. When he'd washed, rinsed and teased her into a shaking mess, Logan pushed her back and hoisted her up.

"Wrap your legs around my waist," he demanded.

She was in the perfect position and he wasted no time slowly slipping his cock through her folds and into her pussy.

"Yes," she hissed in approval.

He pulled out leisurely then paused so he could look her in the eye as he pressed back in.

"So good," she whispered. "Harder."

"Not yet," he scolded. "I'm going to take care of you right."

"You are, you did—please!"

Logan merely buried his face in her neck and continued the torturously leisurely pace. At first, Annabelle fought him. She tried to move her hips faster, but with Logan pinning her to the tiles, she couldn't get the right angle to force his rhythm to change. Eventually, she settled down, allowing him to satisfy her needs.

It wasn't until he felt the tingle at the base of his spine and he was close to release that he sped up. He still took her gently, though. He wanted to prove to her that he'd be sweet and tender, too.

With Annabelle climaxed, she cried out his name. Her body clamped down on his cock almost painfully tightly. He continued thrusting inside, drawing out her pleasure until he came, grunting and shaking.

Annabelle laid her head on his shoulder and sighed. "Wow."

Logan agreed. "Still want to keep doing this?" he teased.

"Oh yeah," she said. "Again and again and again."

"I can't believe that you accept me, as fucked up as I am," Logan whispered.

"Hey." She lifted her head then cupped his face. "That's kind of the normal setting around here. We're all screwed up in one way or another. But you don't have to feel like you have to hide who you really are. No one is going to judge you."

"Maybe they should," he said.

"No one has that right. If I had a chance to do things over, I'd make some better decisions when it came to my safety, but I wouldn't change a thing about what led me here. You were brought to us for a reason. I believe that."

"I think you might be a romantic," Logan teased.

"Shut your mouth," she said with a laugh. "Don't worry too much about why I like you. Just remember that I do."

Chapter Nine

Logan wasn't sure there was enough coffee in the office to keep him awake and focused. He'd had to climb out of Annabelle's bed at six o'clock in order to drive home, shower and get to work on time.

He finished his reports, sent Jamie an email updating him on everything and was now looking into the case files Ruiz had been in charge of. What he was finding did not sit well with Logan. *How has this agent been allowed to run amok?* Logan saved yet another half-finished call log into the secured file on his computer. Ruiz started reports then left them incomplete. Several times, Ruiz had marked the box for follow-up but there'd been no attempt by him to actually do any investigation.

There were already more than thirty problems that Logan had uncovered and he'd only gone through the last two years.

"Such bullshit," he muttered as he transferred the folder onto a USB drive.

Logan couldn't understand why Ruiz had joined the Coalition if he wasn't going to even attempt to do his job. *How did Ruiz even make it past the training, seeing how lazy he is?*

Irritated and tired, Logan yanked free the little device that held his accusations and stood. He'd turn this over to his boss. Commander Parsons was a good agent and leader, but Logan had noticed lately he'd been overwhelmed. As turnover inside the Coalition increased, Parsons had to cover other duties for at least three divisions outside his own. It was time that Logan stepped up and let his boss know what was going on.

He wished he'd paid better attention before. But, keeping himself separate from the other agents, he'd had no idea that Ruiz had been affecting the entire office. That was going to end today.

Logan opened his office door and looked down. Parsons' light was on and the commander was bent over, typing furiously on a laptop. It was now or never. Ruiz hadn't been in the office yet that morning and it was a good time to take Logan's concerns up the chain.

With a casual stride, Logan crossed the bull pen where the newer agents' desks were. Fredrick was at a filing cabinet when Logan passed and Logan nodded to him. Fabian didn't even look up from whatever report he was working on. Logan liked the twins and planned to offer them some help in moving up the ranks.

Even if Fabian was a little too flirty for his taste, the man was smart. He'd handled the transfer of Frank and his cronies, even completing a full write-up of the incident. He was driven and determined, earning Logan's respect.

When Logan reached his boss's office, he rapped sharply on the doorjamb.

"Agent Coldwell." Parson motioned him inside.

Logan stepped across the threshold and into chaos. There were papers, files and old coffee mugs all over the office. He'd never seen the commander's space like this. "Everything okay?" he asked.

Parsons laughed. "There's a method to my madness. Now, what can I do for you?"

Logan slid the USB drive across the desk to Parsons.

His boss picked it up. "And what's this?"

"When I first arrived in Brookside, I met resistance from the local sheriff. It seems he'd been making requests for several months now to our office and is being ignored. I looked into it and it seems that the same agent has received all the calls."

Parsons sighed but nodded. "Let me guess, the agent on

all the reports was Agent Ruiz."

"Yes, sir," Logan responded in surprise.

"I suspended him yesterday," Parsons said. "I'm currently doing an audit of all my agents' cases." He motioned around the room. "And I found issues with Ruiz's." Parsons shook the USB that Logan had given him. "I'll look this over in case I missed anything."

"Oh." Logan was at a loss for words. "Thank you, sir."

"I should have been watching better," Parsons said. "Ruiz was recommended by another commander, so I had assumed he was good at his job. It appears now that the commander was just trying to get rid of his problem by shuffling him over here." Parsons grinned. "I'll be talking to that commander soon as well."

"Sounds like you have everything under control," Logan stated. 'I just wanted to bring this to your attention."

"I know I've been out of the office helping at other divisions and you all have had to fend for yourselves, but there are some changes coming that I think will really help us diversify our staffing and get out and help."

"What do you mean?" Logan asked. He didn't do so well with change. Logan liked routine and order. He was having enough worries about the new state of his personal life to go through a major shake-up at work.

"As the shifter population in this area has decreased, we've seen increases in other locations," Parsons told him.

That was bad news. The commander had to be thinking about transfers, if not closing their office down.

"I can see on your face that you know where this is going," Parsons said.

Logan nodded. He wasn't stupid and if a division was no longer needed there, they'd be moved to an office that was short-staffed.

"One of the reasons I'm auditing all the case files for the past several years is because I need to find agents who will work well on their own."

If there was anything Logan was certain of, it was his

work. He took great pains to make sure that every 'i' was dotted and every 't' was crossed. Parsons wouldn't find the same problems with his paperwork as Logan had seen with Ruiz's. "What did you decide?"

"I've already spoken to several of the senior agents over the last couple of days. You've been working out of the office, but I intended to get a hold of you today," Parsons said.

Even if it meant that he'd screwed up his career, Logan would not apologize for being in Brookside. He'd taken down two separate groups of individuals who would have hurt the residents there. "You're transferring me," Logan said. He didn't need to ask — he knew in his gut.

Parsons nodded. "I was going to move you to the Lake Worth division. Your old academy buddy Jamie Ward said they'd be happy to have you join the feline group. It would have been a real step-up for your career. The Lake Worth division is the biggest and most notable of all Coalition agencies."

"You said you were *going* to transfer me," Logan pointed out. "You're not anymore?" *No,* he silently begged. There was no way that he'd be able to continue seeing Annabelle if he moved to Arizona.

"Another option became available," Parsons told him. "So I'm going to let you pick."

If it was closer to Brookside, then Logan didn't care if they sent him into the middle of nowhere. "Okay."

"I think I know your choice, but I do want to lay out both jobs," Parsons stated.

Logan nodded.

"If you join the feline team in Lake Worth, there will be opportunity for you to lead an entire team within your species. They're promoting some of their team leaders and are in need of strong shifters to fill those roles. It is the best thing for your career. You'll be kept busy and probably get national recognition."

A week ago Logan would have done anything to get the

chance of furthering his career. "My other option?"

"I spoke to the sheriff of Brookside this morning. They've done a great job of keeping an entire town of shifters from the Coalition, but his requests for aid, along with what you've been doing the past several days, have made us re-evaluate that area."

Logan couldn't believe it. Was the perfect job posting really just falling into his lap? "I see."

"You'd be the senior agent in Brookside and, while I can move a couple junior agents with you, for the most part you'd be on your own. You'd still get support from the closest Coalition agency, but you'll office within the sheriff's department and work hand in hand with the local force."

It was really hard for Logan to remain stoic when he wanted to jump for joy.

"I can give you a couple of days to decide, but this office will be closing within two weeks."

"I don't need a couple of weeks," Logan assured his boss.

"I didn't think you would," Parsons said, but he appeared somewhat disappointed.

"I'll take the position in Brookside," Logan announced. The words felt so good coming out of his mouth. No more having to worry about the commute. He already cared about the residents of the small town. And best of all, he might have Annabelle in his bed every night.

Parsons blinked at him. "What?"

"Brookside," Logan repeated.

"I... I didn't expect you to choose that one," Parsons admitted. He shuffled a few papers on his desk, which seemed unusual.

That was when he it hit Logan. "You didn't expect it, but it's what you wanted?" he guessed.

Parsons looked up at him. "Honestly?"

Logan nodded. He was really curious to see what his boss had to stay.

"Yes, I think that Lake Worth would be best for your career, but I don't think it would best for you," Parsons said.

"Okay." Logan leaned forward, intrigued.

"You're one of the best agents who have ever worked under me. You didn't join the Coalition for fame. You wanted to make a difference," Parson said. "I think you could do that better in Brookside. They really need someone who will look out for their needs. If I put another agent there, I'm not sure that they'd connect the same as you seem to have."

"I agree," Logan said. "I was comfortable there. Had a lot in common with the shifters I met. I don't need to move up the chain of command. I just need to be able to do my job."

"I haven't been so pleasantly surprised in such a long time," Parsons told him.

"What about Olivia?" Logan asked. His partner had been off for a while on personal leave, but he didn't want to leave her to fend for herself.

"I spoke to her yesterday. She hadn't been certain she would be able to come here. She really is needed at home."

Logan had been worried about that. Olivia had kept pushing back her return date.

"There's an office in the city where her parents live and they had one opening. She accepted the position," Parsons informed him. "I asked her not to tell you until I'd had a chance to give you the news myself."

"I'm glad she can stay by her family," Logan said sincerely.

"Since you're going to take the Brookside position, I'm happy to say that I'll still be your commander. You'll send me all your reports. It'll be a little longer for help, since the closest division will be over two hours away now, but the sheriff is willing to make any changes to his department for the joint calibration."

"It sounds good to me. You said I'd have access to junior agents?"

"Yes," Parson confirmed. "With the number of residents concentrated in that one area, I can give you part-time help. They'd be on call, again a couple of hours from you, but they'll also be available to work with you three to four times a week."

"Can I make a request of who it might be?"

"Sure," Parsons replied. "I didn't think you were close to any of the younger agents."

"I'm not," he admitted. "But if Fredrick and Fabian are available, I wouldn't mind working with them again. They've shown initiative and drive. The experience of working with different species would be good training."

"Ah." Parsons smiled. "The wonder twins. Yes, I think it would do them some good and they'll be happy to hear it. I'll see what I can work out."

Pleased with the way the morning had gone, Logan relaxed. He wasn't used to things working out in his favor. Struggling and always having to make his own way had hardened him, but Logan was getting a new chance at life. So many opportunities were coming at him. It was almost overwhelming.

"Now start packing up your office and get out of here. You look beat down," Parsons ordered.

Laughing, he nodded. "It's been a rough few days, but I've got to admit I've enjoyed it."

"Good." Parsons stood and held out his hand. "I'll be in touch."

He rose and shook the hand of the man he really admired. Logan was thankful that Parsons hadn't just assumed he'd want to go to Lake Worth. By being given the choice, Logan had changed the direction he'd been headed in and couldn't be happier. He was excited to tell Annabelle about the changes.

There was still some uncertainly about their relationship. Logan was going to have to find a place to live, because it was probably too soon to move in with Annabelle, but just being in the same town was going to alter how they approached things.

As he left Parsons' office, he fingered his cell in his pocket. He could call her, but he'd much rather give her the news in person.

At the threshold of his office, he peered around the room. He hadn't personalized the space. On Olivia's side, she had pictures of her family and loved ones. He'd never had any he could put up, so Logan hadn't decorated at all. Maybe Annabelle would help him set up his new office and he could snap a photo of them to hang.

He'd need just one small box to get his belongings home. His apartment would be a little harder to pack up, but Logan now knew a few strong shifters who he didn't think would mind helping him out.

Logan spun on his heel to head to the supply closet to get a box and collided with Fabian.

"Hey, Logan," Fabian said, more reserved than Logan had ever heard.

"How's it going?" he asked.

"Good." Fabian looked past him into Logan's office. "Do you need any help?"

"No, man," Logan slapped his shoulder. "I don't have hardly anything."

"Oh."

"Isn't everything okay?" Logan asked the younger shifter.

"Did you really request me and Fredrick?"

Was that not what Fabian wanted? He hadn't meant to step on anyone's toes or mess up their assignments. "Is that a problem? I can ask Parsons to reconsider."

"No!" Fabian practically shouted. He cleared his throat then spoke more quietly. "No, we don't want that."

"I'm sorry. I don't understand what is happening here," Logan admitted.

"This morning we got our new postings and we were getting separated. I know that's always a possibility and we've been lucky so far, but I wasn't prepared for it. Fredrick is more than my brother. He's my twin, I'm connected to him in a way that I can't explain."

Logan nodded, not really sure what to say.

"Parsons said since you requested us, we'd be able to

office at the same division when not with you. We might have to work separate cases, which is okay, but we'd still be together," Fabian said. "They were going to send us to different states."

"Then I'm glad I was able to change that. But I'll work you hard and I'm a stickler for reports. If you do it wrong, I will make you redo the paperwork until I think it's right."

"We're not afraid of hard work," Fabian stated with pride. "And we studied all the senior agents' reports when we first got here. Yours are always the best and we already use your system."

"Good." Logan appreciated the compliment. "Then I look forward to working more with you."

"So when do we start?" Fabian asked.

"First thing Monday morning I want you both to be in Brookside. I'll be set up by then and we'll be getting caught up on the cases that the sheriff normally has to deal with. I'll also set up a meeting for the afternoon with the Park service. We're going to be working closely with the two departments to keep safe not only the Brookside residents, but all the tourists who go to see the forest."

Fabian nodded before sending Logan his customary cocky grin. "Shouldn't be a problem. I plan to still be in town for my date this weekend, anyway."

Yeah, the kid was going to be just fine.

And so was Logan.

* * * *

Annabelle looked over her favorite branch into the yard below. From her tree, she could see the entire back part of the bar. Duffy and Calvin were doing maintenance on their bikes as Mac, Trent, Carter and Kelly sat talking and laughing around a picnic table that they'd moved out there earlier.

The barbecue grill that Trent had shown up with was smoking, sending the aroma of cooking meat into the air.

Her stomach was already growling as she lounged up high.

It wasn't often they had a lazy afternoon just for themselves, but Mac had insisted after the mess with the fox troop the night before. No one had been seriously injured, but they'd all been scared. So they were taking time together, just enjoying themselves. Annabelle had immediately shifted and headed to her spot. She'd socialize later, but right then she wanted to lie back in the sunlight that beamed down on her.

Annabelle closed her eyes and sighed. The only person missing from the day was Logan. He'd had to go back to work and Annabelle wasn't sure when she'd see him again. Logan had promised to call after he'd kissed her goodbye, but Annabelle knew he had to be tired.

Part of the reason she'd decided to nap in her tree was because she hadn't been able to get back to sleep after Logan had left. How often was she going to have to watch him leave for work and not know when she'd see him again? She wasn't used to not having the people she wanted to talk to right there.

Since she didn't have a choice, Annabelle was going to have to get past the feeling of disappointment. Logan liked his job and she wouldn't stand in the way of that. There'd be times when she needed to help someone and wouldn't be available to him. They'd work it out. They had to.

Keeping her eyes closed, Annabelle rolled over onto her back, lifting her legs into the air. The warmth from the day beat down on her and she meowed happily. She let the sounds of her surroundings trickle to the back of her consciousness. *What a perfect afternoon.*

The murmur of voices remained quiet enough that she felt connected to her family while still able to daydream. She hoped that over the weekend Logan might want to shift together. Annabelle was curious to see him as a lion and she didn't think that her margay was going to have a problem transforming with him. Hell, she was on the verge of falling in love with him. Who would have thought that he'd have been Annabelle's type? Logan was picky, a little on the stuffy side, with a clean-cut image. He was also powerful, dominant and bossy. The perfect combination.

"Are you really asleep up there?"

Annabelle blinked open her eyes before rolling over to look below. She wasn't certain that she was really seeing him. She yowled at him in question.

Logan laughed, waving her down. "Yes, I'm really here," he said. "Now come here."

With great effort, she pulled herself from her nest and started down head-first.

"Wow!" Logan exclaimed.

Because of her flexible ankles, Annabelle was one of the few feline species that could pull off that move. It helped when hunting in the trees.

"That's unbelievable," Logan praised.

Halfway down the trunk, Annabelle stopped hanging on by her claws. Logan would probably catch her if she leaped at him. Even if he missed, she wouldn't hurt herself landing on the ground.

"Really?" he said. "You want to jump on me?"

She really did.

He sighed long and loud, but the smile on his face gave away his true feelings. "Fine."

Pushing off with her powerful back legs, Annabelle launched herself at him. Logan opened his arms and she landed easily within his embrace. She made sure to have her claws retracted so as not to injure him.

Logan immediately lifted her up and nuzzled the top of her head. She purred, loving the sweet gesture.

"I like seeing you like this," Logan said. He began walking over to the picnic table and was greeted warmly by the others.

"We didn't expect you so soon," Mac commented.

"I know." He ran his finger under her chin and Annabelle was in heaven. She wiggled around enough that she could bare her belly to him, silently asking for a good rub there.

"I had something to talk to Annabelle about."

She stiffened.

"Shh, it's okay." Logan did caress her belly. "Nothing bad, I promise."

With a quick swipe of her paw, she was able to wrap it around his wrist and pull his hand to her mouth. Annabelle had learned how to communicate as a margay since she loved shifting so much.

"Ouch." Logan pulled his thumb away after her tooth dug deep. "It's not bad!"

Guess I'll have to wait and see.

Mac and Trent were chuckling, but Annabelle hadn't been trying to be cute. She was giving Logan a warning. Things were going well for them and an unexpected visit in the middle of the day didn't bode well.

"I'm going to take her inside so she can shift where we'll be able to talk," Logan said.

"I don't know," Trent replied. "At least this way, she can't argue back."

Annabelle hissed at him.

"Hey." Logan thumbed her nose and she blinked at him in surprise. There was no way he'd just done that. She wasn't an actual housecat.

Trent was laughing so hard that he almost fell off the bench. Even if it came at her expense, she liked seeing him so happy.

"Go on," Mac said. "We still have a good while before the food's ready. If you don't return we'll put the leftovers in the kitchen."

"Eww," Carter bitched. "Did you really need to say that?"

"Like you didn't know what they were going to be doing," Trent teased.

"We don't need to talk about it!" Carter cried.

Annabelle knew that Carter was only playing around, so she swiped out as though she was going to claw at him. Logan pulled her back against his chest, though. She didn't mind, since that put her close to the muscles she enjoyed so much.

"Come on, hellcat," Logan murmured to her as he carried her toward the back entrance.

She didn't know what he needed to talk to her about, but she wasn't going to freak. No matter what he said, there had to be a way to make things work. Logan was still nuzzling her as he meandered down the hall to her room. He opened the door and gave her a kiss on her nose before dropping her onto the bed.

"I really do need to talk to you."

Annabelle began her transformation back to human. It was easier for her than some of the others, since she made sure to change at least once a day. The longer a shifter went without transforming, the longer it took. The change didn't hurt. It was just a little uncomfortable.

In just a few moments, she was on her back in the middle of her bed, peering up at a grinning Logan. If he was this happy, then his news couldn't be too terrible.

"Okay, clothes," he said. Logan bent to pick up the sweatpants and tank she'd discarded earlier.

"What, you don't want me naked?" she teased.

He threw the clothing at her. "Not yet."

"Fine." Giving him her best pout, Annabelle dressed. Once she was covered up, she glared at him. "Happy now?"

"I can't wait to take them back off."

She tossed her hands up in the air. "Really?"

Logan sat in the chair across from the bed.

"You're not going to even sit next to me?"

"No way I'd be able to keep my hands off you."

Well, that was a little better. "What happened?"

Logan leaned forward, bracing his forearms on his knees. "The division of my office is closing."

"They're moving you?" she asked. "I thought that you said it wasn't bad news?"

"I was given two choices. The first was to go to the largest Coalition office as a feline team leader."

"In Arizona?" She knew where he was talking about.

They'd had a lot of high-profile cases. That would be really good for Logan, but it was so far away.

"The other is right here," Logan said.

"Here? Where?"

"In Brookside."

"We don't have a Coalition agency in town."

"Magnus has been having some issues lately and he spoke to my boss about getting some support here. My commander offered to allow me to office inside the sheriff's department."

"You'd stay here permanently?" *Dare I hope?* "But what about the other offer?"

"It would be great for my career," Logan said. "I won't lie about that, but it doesn't have what's most important to me."

"And what's that?" She was almost afraid to ask.

"You."

"You'd give up a dream job for me?" she questioned. "That only happens in romance novels."

"No," he said. "I'm not giving up anything. By taking the posting here, I'll get to work with men that I admire. I'll have the chance to get to know everyone better. Like I told you before, I feel comfortable here and I've never had that anywhere else. But the biggest attraction is being in the same place as you."

"You sound like you already made your decision."

"I have," Logan said. "This is where I want to be."

Brookside was where she wanted him to be, but that wasn't best for his career. "What if it doesn't work out between us?" She had to state her real concern.

"I don't know," he said quietly. "I would hope that we'd still be friends and I could stay here. It's a risk, I know. One that I'm not sure will work out in the end, but if I go to Arizona, I know I won't have what might happen for me here. I want a family and yours seems to be accepting of me. You are who I want to spend my time with. I want to learn every little thing about you."

"Wow," she whispered, trying to hold back her emotions.

"A good wow?" he asked. "Because I need you to tell me how you feel. This is a big step for us. If you don't want to go further in our relationship, I need to know."

"I want you." She moved to her knees and shuffled down to the end of the bed so she was right in front of him. "I want us."

Logan relaxed his shoulders and he ran his hands over his face then smiled at her. "I didn't think I was going to be so nervous. I practiced what I would say the entire drive here."

"I can't believe it. It's like everything that I want is just within my reach."

"That's exactly how I feel. So I'm staying and you're going to have to help me house hunt."

Annabelle looked around her bedroom.

"I don't think we should move in together after just one date," he quipped.

Annabelle laughed. "Doesn't it seem like so much longer?"

He was already nodding before she'd even finished her sentence. "I can't seem to remember my life before I met you. I don't ever want to go back to that again."

"You don't have to." She climbed off the bed and into his lap. "Even if something happened between us, you'll always have this weird, overly protective, crazy group of shifters that have your back."

Logan stood. "Right now I'm more concerned about getting you on *your* back."

"Oh yeah?" She ran her palm over his chest.

"Yep!" Logan tossed her in the air and she flew to the head of the bed. He quickly covered her body with his as he brought his lips against hers.

Annabelle gripped the short hair at the back of his head. She wondered briefly if he'd consider growing his hair out but all thought left her when he snaked his hand up her top.

She ripped her mouth away and rolled him until she was on top. Rocking her hips so that his cock was trapped under her, she pushed at the material over his shoulders. Logan rose briefly to help her get the shirt off him then flopped back down.

The need to taste him overwhelmed her. She ran her hands over every piece of his flesh before she tugged at his slacks. It was a race to get both of them undressed so she'd feel him buried inside her once again.

"I want you to ride me just like this."

Annabelle reached back and grasped his erection, positioning it at the entrance of her pussy. "I want it hard," she told him.

"You control the pace, baby," he said. "Take what you want."

Slowly, she lowered herself down. Logan kept his gaze on hers and she saw the affection and caring in the depths of his eyes. He looked at her like she was the best thing that had ever happened to him.

Leaning down to kiss him, she lifted up on her knees then slid back down. Logan gripped her hips and bucked up, driving his cock in farther. She moaned into his mouth.

She braced herself with her hands on his pecs. Annabelle threw her head back and started to ride him the way that they both wanted. Slow and sweet had been great the night before, but this time their lovemaking was full of heat and need.

Annabelle let her body naturally fall into its rhythm until Logan began to plunge up fast and hard. She was shaking, bouncing around on his cock, and it was marvelous. She glanced down at him and got to witness the pure pleasure on his features. Clamping her inner muscles down on his shaft drew a long, low groan, so she did it again and again.

Logan clenched his teeth while bracing his feet on the mattress and began to plow into her. Annabelle grasped her breasts, which were shaking with Logan's hard thrusts, and thumbed at her nipples.

The zing went down her stomach and all the way to her clit.

She dropped down, rolled her hips and came. With a cry, she exploded into climax, drawing a series of grunts from Logan.

He rolled them until he was on top then grabbed her leg, spreading her wide to plunge deep. She was panting, trying to find something to hold on to — anything to hold on to. Logan growled then stilled as he reached orgasm.

Annabelle watched every second of his release. His cheeks were flushed and sweat beaded his brow. He blinked his open eyes and smiled.

She lifted, allowing his cock to slip out. Annabelle dropped down beside him to cuddle against his side.

"It keeps getting better and better," he murmured.

"I agree."

Logan ran his hand gently over her side while she gazed up at him. An idea began to form and she didn't know if she should bring it up. Hell, why shouldn't she?

"I know of a house you can rent," she told him.

"You do?" he asked, propping his head up on a bended arm.

"It's halfway between the bar and town. It would be perfect for you. A small two-bedroom, two-bath, but the back yard is gorgeous."

"You think the owner would rent it to me?" he asked.

She turned her head and kissed right above his heart. "Yes. I think she might like you more than just a little bit."

"You own a house?" he guessed with a laugh.

"Yep," she confirmed. "Mac helped me buy it several years ago. I planned to move in one day, but so far I haven't had the urge to leave this place. Duffy and Calvin keep talking about moving above the tattoo shop and Kelly is looking for an apartment. Sooner or later, I figure we won't all live here and didn't want to be left all alone."

"You'll never be alone," he assured her.

"I know that in my heart, but sometimes I think too much about how things could change." She sighed. "I might want my own house eventually, anyway. I really like it. Did I mention the trees in the back yard?"

"No," Logan said. "But I get the feeling that was a major buying feature."

"It was," Annabelle admitted. "If I wasn't afraid to be alone, then I'd have already moved in."

Logan rubbed his chin over the top of her head. "Maybe you just needed someone to share it with."

Annabelle nodded. "You could stay there and we'll have sleepovers and fix the place up. It's been empty a long time."

"Then maybe someday you'll move in with me," he said.

"It's a possibility. That is, if you still want to be associated with me. Once word gets out around town about us, you'll probably get some weird looks. I'm an oddity even among felines."

"Trust me," Logan told her. "I'll be very proud to let everyone know that you belong to me and me alone."

"Maybe we could shift later?" she asked quietly. "If that would be okay?"

"Are you kidding?" Logan said with excitement. "I've been itching to shift for a while and I'd love you run with you. Although you have to give me a head start if you're going to be jumping from tree to tree."

"I'll think about it," Annabelle teased. "It depends on how good a boy you are."

Logan rolled her to her back before covering her body with his. He peered down at her with heat in his eyes. "When we're out in the woods, I'm going to mark our spot from last night. Everyone who passes by will know that I claimed you there."

Annabelle grinned. "Claim me here first."

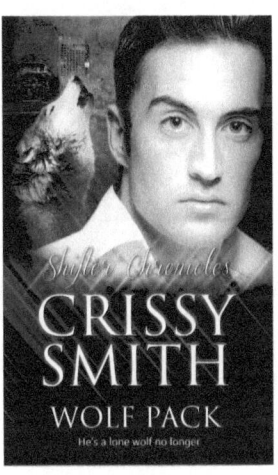

Wolf Pack

Excerpt

Chapter One

Loud, echoing footsteps bounced off the small stairway as Kendra Brown's adrenaline pulsed through her body. Sweat dripped down her neck as the tactical vest overheated her. She gripped her weapon tighter and smiled. It was time. Kendra followed behind the Lake Worth SWAT team as they led the way up the back stairway to the fifth floor of the old, run-down motel. Uniformed police were watching the front as well as surrounding the outside completely.

Her office had gotten a tip that the missing witness she'd been searching for was holed up in room five-eleven.

That was her mission today. She needed to bring in Trent Compton and protect him, even if it was against himself. Trent's life had changed forever when he'd seen his boss kill two men. He'd done the right thing and called the police after he'd gotten away. An investigation had followed and the Marshals had set Trent up in a safe house with protection.

The plan had worked until two days ago, when the two Marshals assigned to Trent had been killed and Trent had disappeared. One of the agents had managed to send an emergency text to their superiors asking for help, but by the time local officers had arrived at the safe house it had been too late for them.

She gripped her weapon harder as she paused behind the officer who had stopped on the stair above her. The SWAT leader was at the door to the hall, holding up five fingers. Silently he counted down, one finger falling at a time, until he held up only a fist. At that, another officer threw open the door and they filed in, fast and efficient.

Kendra followed at their heels but made sure to remain out of the way. She braced her shoulders against the far wall. One officer held up a battering ram and with his feet braced apart he swung it back then hit the door to the motel room. It broke open, splintering, and wood flew in all different directions. She flinched away as the SWAT team rushed forward into the room. They moved quietly, and Kendra felt disappointment course through her when she didn't hear any orders to get down.

Since the Marshal's office didn't run the same way that most law-enforcement agencies did, Kendra had learned early in her career to work with others. When something like breaching an entrance was needed, she had to join a joint task force. She didn't mind — unlike some federal and local badges. Most other agencies treated the Marshals like they were less but for the most part Kendra had teamed with really good agents and officers who wanted to catch the bad guys. And that was what Kendra did best — witness protection and finding people on the run.

She pushed herself off the wall before she slowly made her way to the entry. She held up her weapon and peeked around the splintered frame. The team were glancing around and searching the bathroom and closet, but Kendra already knew that the place was empty.

The manager of the motel had confirmed that he'd rented a room to Trent but he hadn't been able to say when the last time was that he'd spotted him. Kendra had wanted to wait until she'd confirmed that he was still inside but she'd been overruled by the local captain. Captain Villa, the SWAT boss, had been in charge of this particular operation and was one of the cops who had a problem working with the Marshals. Because of the man's prejudice against her agency, Kendra had lost her best lead on Trent.

"Fuck," she spat but walked through the old dirty space. There were empty pizza boxes, beer bottles and other trash. She didn't spot any clothes, though. She strolled over to the drawers and yanked them open. Empty. She left them hanging open before stomping to the bathroom. It was filthy, but she didn't feel any moisture in the air, so it must have been a while since it'd been used.

When she walked back into the bedroom she wasn't surprised that most of the team had moved to the hallway and only the SWAT leader remained.

"I'm sorry," Sergeant Matthews told her.

She could hear the sincerity in his voice. While his captain had been a complete ass, Matthews seemed like a solid officer and had been willing to listen to her when she'd wanted to wait to verify that Trent was still inside.

Now they'd lost the only connection to Trent.

Kendra shrugged before she rolled her neck around, trying to let go of her aggravation. It wouldn't be easy to track down Trent again but she was good at her job. "Can you give me a minute?"

"Sure." He nodded before he left the room.

She didn't really mind if anyone was in the room with her as she let a little of her animal side out, so the sergeant could have stayed, but she didn't want any other scents distracting her. She'd mastered bringing the wolf to the edge without fully shifting. It did freak some people out but Kendra didn't give a shit. Humans could either accept her or get out of her way. Her kind had been hidden for way too long.

When all of the shifter species had united and decided to announce their presence, Kendra had been thrilled. She'd hated hiding who and what she was. Her parents had lived in fear for almost all their lives. They hadn't known what to do with such a headstrong, independent daughter.

Luck had been on her side when her parents had reached out to the Alpha and he'd taken her under his wing. She owed him so much, and he was one of the reasons that it was so important that Trent was found and all the attacks stopped. She had to get answers.

Kendra stepped closer to the unmade bed. She breathed in deeply as she dropped to her knees. Through the sweat, old food and stale beer, she could pick up on the scent that was unique to Trent. His clothing had been provided in an evidence bag with his file so she could determine that Trent had been in the room. He had been, but the scent was at least twenty-four hours old. The foul aroma of fear was heavy in the room. Something had made Trent flee from this room, and Kendra didn't believe it was her search for him. No, Trent had some bad people after him and if Kendra didn't find him first there was a good chance she wouldn't get to see him alive.

Once she was she was sure she had all she could get from the scene, she stiffened her shoulders and turned to stroll out of the door.

Matthews was leaning against the wall with his ankles crossed while texting on his phone. He glanced up when she joined him.

"I have a buddy that works for the Shifter Coalition. I asked him if I could give you his contact information and he said sure. I know this sting was fucked up and I feel real bad about that," Matthews told her.

She nodded. "I appreciate that. Too bad your captain doesn't feel the same."

Matthews sighed before he slipped his phone into his

pocket. "He doesn't like feds, and the fact that you're a shifter?" Matthews scoffed. "There was no way that he'd listen to you."

Kendra wasn't surprised anymore about how people acted but it still pissed her off. "I'll deal with him now."

The smile that spread across Matthews' face was evil. "Can I watch?"

She laughed. As much as Kendra wished she could shift and teach the captain a real lesson, her Alpha wouldn't approve. But she could give the captain a piece of her mind. She only played nice for so long. Captain Villa was about to find out why she was the best Marshal in the area.

More books from
Crissy Smith

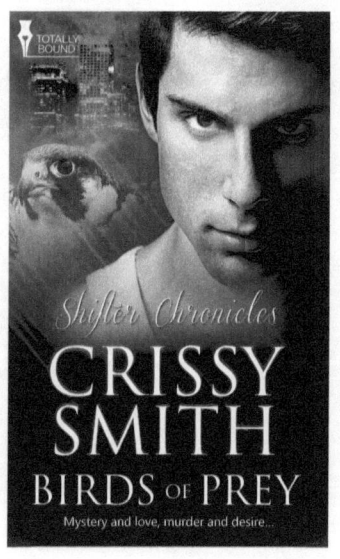

Book one in the Shifter Chronicles series

Mystery and love, murder and desire… It's going to be a rough week for the agents of the Birds of Prey shifter division.

Book one in the Were Chronicles series

Marissa Boyd finds herself drawn into a world she can never be a part of, complete with an Alpha wolf who takes whatever he wants. And he wants her.

Book four in the Were Chronicles series

The Rogue meets the Alpha…and their worlds explode.

Book one in the Bloodlines series

If trouble doesn't come to him, he'll find it on his own.

About the Author

Crissy Smith

Crissy Smith lives in Texas with her husband, daughter, and three Labrador retrievers. The three dogs love to curl up under her computer desk and nap while she writes. It doesn't leave a lot of room for her but what's a woman to do?

When not writing or reading, she enjoys hunting, camping and shooting. But she has a girly side too and is addicted to pedicures and coffee.

She has been writing since she was a teenager and still loves everything to do with the paranormal. Her stories and characters all have a place in her heart. She loves the alpha male, the dominant werewolf, or the Master vampire which find their way in most of her books.

Learn more about the characters she has created at her website where they have their very own page. It will be updated from time to time to let you know what's going on with them. You can also find out who will be in the next book.

Crissy Smith loves to hear from readers. You can find contact information, website details and an author profile page at https://www.totallybound.com/